D1706980

Dedications

In Loving Memory of Our Parents

Bryan William Hurt

October 1, 1933-July 1, 2015

Bobbie Brannon Pate Hurt

July 23, 1935-February 2, 2015

The best examples of true dedication to family

You taught us the true meaning of love

In Loving Memory of My Mother-in-Law

Margaret K. Rainey

December 6, 1929-January 10, 1993

My mentor, best friend and "fishing buddy"

Thank you for loving me as your own

Special thanks to Perry G. Green D.M.D.

Major U.S.A.F (retired)

The true test of a friend is when help is given without benefit of spoken word

The cover photo is courtesy of ©By böhringer friedrich (Own work) [CC BY-SA 2.5 (http://creativecommons.org/licenses/by-sa/2.5)], via Wikimedia Commons and makes no endorsements for the book or any part thereof. This wonderful vintage truck from the past is a Kenworth model W900, a prized possession of many contractors of the book's time period. It is also the same truck Hammer Lane drives in the book.

Hammer Lane Express is a fictional work. Any similarities to persons either living or deceased are purely coincidental unless otherwise mentioned or stated.

Exception made in the honor of and commitment made to Ursula, beloved waitress and community diplomat of the Bee Bayou Truck Stop of Bee Bayou, Louisiana. I told you I would write a book with you in it one day as you are held in high esteem among your drivers and friends. A beacon in the night for the weary truck driver your comedic personality can never be duplicated as a truer friend in the trucking world there has never been. We all love and respect you greatly.

Contents

Introduction

With the help of an independent maverick truck driver known as Bob, Mike Turner takes on a new career as a long distance trucker. He quickly begins to question what he believed to be the correct decision for his family when uncertainty, confusion and frustration become his constant companion. He then learns there may be more secrecy surrounding Bob than meets the eye as shadowy events surrounding a dead truck driver slowly come to light. He must determine whether Bob is the angel sent from God his family believes him to be. Or could there be another unknown agenda hidden beneath the dark tinted sunglasses covering the eyes of a badly disfigured face? Mystery runs deep and wild as you ride along with the drivers of Hammer Lane Express.

The time period for this book is the mid nineteen eighties. A time of turmoil and uncertainty in trucking and continues today. Some say it is because of deregulation of the trucking industry shortly before this time period. For those who don't know, prior to this the ICC (Interstate Commerce Commission) regulated all trucking and assigned designated routes to travel and the type of freight they could haul. All freight went one way and the truck once unloaded could only go back to where he started empty unless they were to trip lease to another carrier. Only a few carriers had the rights to haul back to their home area. The ICC was abolished and The FMCSA (Federal Motor Carrier Safety Administration) became the new governing body. Who is to say maybe it's a sign of the times or perhaps a sign of the times yet to come. Enjoy the ride.

Hammer Lane Express

On the Fast Lane of Life

Chapter One

The Rookie

The tall Georgia pines cast a long dark shadow over the graveled parking lot of the old truck stop as the dark green Peterbilt 359 rolled off of the pavement then slowly by the fuel islands. Mike was amazed how easily John controlled the oversize load of steel plates around obstacles and through the pot hole abundant lot. He then pulled into a parking spot with the precision which only comes from many years of experience. John pulled the parking brakes making a popping sound proclaiming proudly to the world this day was officially completed. He settled back into the seat then looked around the heavily worn parking lot and asked his trainee, Mike.

"Think you learned anything new today, rookie?"

Mike is a young man in his early 30's. This will be his first trucking experience, yet he couldn't help but wonder where it may lead. He is a God loving man with a beautiful wife, two handsome boys and a sparkling little girl. Cautiously, he was starting a new career, one he hoped would allow him to provide much better for his family. Already he is questioning his own decision.

"Yeah, there's more to it than I thought there would be."

Mike held back what he wanted to say so badly. The one most important being, "Don't call me rookie, mister!"

John shrugged his shoulders as if he actually heard Mike's last thought. After many years of training drivers for the company, perhaps he did.

"Get your gear and let's go check into the motel, daylight will come early."

John opened the door, turned around and stepped down. John is an older driver with over 20 years of driving experience. A no nonsense type person with very little patience for the weak minded. This will be one of many he was given the responsibility of forging into a truck driver for the company. He didn't know how to explain why he continued to do it, perhaps as a favor to the owner, Mary.

As Mike walked slowly along he noticed with great interest all the different types of trucks parked on the lot and wondered where they were destined. He questioned what was concealed behind doors, inside tanks and also under tarpaulins. Most of the engines were idling to keep the cab cool for the driver's comfort. A few were running to keep their pet cool while they patiently waited for their master to return. For a moment he pondered why would anyone want to carry a dog or a cat with them in a truck? It was a simple question and one would to be answered beyond reason in time. With the diesel engines rumbling and all of the different sizes, the many odd shapes plus the sheer number of trucks on the lot Mike imagined he was back in another time among the dinosaurs. They appeared to surround him as they settled in for a long night rest. With first light they will awake and roam the earth again with each choosing a different path of travel. It had been an eventful first day. Perhaps some time to let the events settle in was required for now. The one thing he fully believed at this very moment, it was not at all how he thought trucking would be.

"Hello John, same room as usual?" asked the motel manager.

"Same I guess set it up for two."

John filled out the registration then gave the keys to Mike.

"How about taking your and my gear to the room and meet me in the restaurant, rookie?"

Mike grabbed the bags and continued to the room thinking I've had just about enough of this rookie crap. He unlocked the room door then walked in and took a look around. Sadly, there was not much to see. There were two twin beds, a table and two chairs and small bath/shower room just big enough for one person to enter and use. There was not even a window, only a hole cut into the wall with a window heat and a/c unit installed. As he looked around the room he felt a loneliness he never felt before he found very hard to explain. At first he thought it must be he was missing his family and home, but there was so much more. For the first time in his life he could relate to someone who lived in a lesser country. They probably dreamed of coming to America for a better and richer life. Once here they soon realized things are a little different than the New World of their dreams. To turn back now would be admitting failure and defeat. This was simply not acceptable because there were others to consider. Mike realized more than ever how much his family depended on him to succeed. He tossed the bags on the bed and walked out locking the door.

"What can I get for you, John?"

The waitress smiled as John sat down. He glanced at her a moment then replied, "Give me a while. I've got a trainee with me and waiting on him to get here."

"Sure thing sweetie, I'll be back later." She then walked off to check on other customers.

Mike sat down across from John and picked up the menu as he looked around at the restaurant. There was a long service bar with individual stools that went maybe twenty feet or so then made a turn and went back again leaving room for the waitress to walk through the middle and work both sides. Toward the center were a few tables with seating for six. Along the walls were about fifteen or twenty booths where four people could sit. This was one of which John and Mike occupied. It was very noisy as dishes and silverware are rattling and the jukebox is on high volume playing country music. Very distracting as well were the drivers talking so loudly as though they were trying to get the attention of everyone in the room. There was also the occasional intercom announcement paging a driver to the fuel desk for a phone call from their dispatch. It was quite a difference from the cab of the truck where you could control the noise somewhat should you desire.

"Decided what you want?" the waitress inquired of John.

"Think I'll have a hamburger steak with fries and coffee."

"And you dear?" looking at Mike.

"Spaghetti and a soda," replied Mike hoping he made the right choice. This would be his first meal in a truck stop. He glanced around still taking in this new culture surrounding him. He felt like a child who was on his first outing with his parents to a new restaurant. Everything caught his attention, even the ceiling fans!

"Coming right up," she remarked as she walked away.

John looked over at Mike, "Ever eat at a buffet before, rookie?"

Mike decided for now he would let the rookie comment slide. "A buffet, what the heck is a buffet?"

John gazed at Mike for a moment, "Boy, you must have led a sheltered life. Some places up north call them a smorgasbord. It's a long hot bar set up with different types of foods. You go and help yourself for one price and eat all you want. It's sort of like a church social dinner or family reunion."

Mike thought about it for a moment and then chuckled, "I don't think it will work in the South. There are too many people who could eat them right out of business," then shook his head.

Mike snickered again, "I doubt you will ever see any buffets around here, John."

Then the waitress brought their food and they began to eat. After the meal they got up from the table leaving a tip and paid the bill at the register. As they were at the register an older driver came up and made a strange remark to John, "I see they'll let just about anyone in here now."

John turned around, "No, just me!" John giggled, "How have you been doing Hot Rod, are you still driving the cab over Freight Shaker?"

The man smiled widely. "Makes just as much money as any other truck out here, it takes a little less money to do it with you know. Still training drivers for the boss lady?"

John looked down shaking his head. "Yeah, we keep training them. Then they go somewhere else to drive."

The driver shook his head, "Maybe you should stop running them off, John. Then you could stop having to replace them so often."

They laughed hardily as they patted one another's back and then walked away.

"That a friend of yours?" inquired Mike.

"Yeah, I've known that cantankerous old driver for so long I've forgotten his name. I just call him by his CB handle, Hot Rod. We drove for a company out of Birmingham years ago. Some of the best people I've ever known drove there such as Hot Rod, Dixie Flash, Blue Moon, Hammer Lane…," at which point Mike hastily broke in.

"You drove with Hammer Lane, the actual Hammer Lane!"

Puzzled, John answered, "Sure did, why?"

Mike looked John directly in the eyes, "At the truck driving school I went to he was sort of a legend, but not a good one!"

John, having to know more queried.

"A legend you say and just what kind of legend?"

Mike explained to John, “In the truck driving school the instructors taught the right way to drive and conduct your actions. They used the exploits of Hammer Lane as examples of the wrong way to drive and what not to do.”

John listened long as he could stand as apparently this touched a sore nerve with him. Then he quickly broke in, “Hammer was a really close friend of mine and not a legend. I think we've talked about this long enough!” Then he walked off toward the motel room.

Mike wasn’t sure what apparently happened. Somehow he unintentionally upset John badly. Therefore he must surely know more about this man called Hammer Lane. This man he was led to believe was the worst thing to happen to the trucking world since the invention of the wheel. Was it possible the instructors at the driving school were wrong?

As Mike walked into the room John was already taking his clothes off to take a shower before bed.

John glanced at Mike and in a matter of fact way barked out, “It doesn't matter to me, but if you're not comfortable with watching me undress you can go out to the lounge or wherever you want.”

Not sure what to do Mike replied, “Nah, doesn’t bother me if it doesn't bother you.”

John just nodded and proceeded to undress. Mike stretched out on the bed and was thinking what have I gotten myself into? John began taking off his pants. He wore boxer type shorts and Mike couldn't help noticing his right leg was mutilated badly from his foot up along his side and up to his underwear, perhaps further. He knew John appeared to walk with a slight limp, but didn't realize until now how serious it could actually be. Remembering the earlier conversation over Hammer Lane he was not sure if he should ask about the leg. So for now he would let it slide along with the rookie comments.

John slipped into the shower and drew the curtain behind.

Hammer Lane Express

Mike lay back on the bed listening to the sounds around him. The faint sound of the juke box in the lounge, the rumble of a truck either entering or leaving the parking lot and of course the soothing sound of the shower water splashing along the curtain. It was the aroma of the motel soap and shampoo which reminded him so much of home. He reminisced how he would relax on the bed while waiting for his wife to finish her bath before sleep each night. It had been a long day and it was taking its toll. His thoughts of home soon consumed his soul so strongly that little, by little, by little…

"Best go ahead and take a shower since I don't know when we will get another chance. You sure went to sleep fast last night. You were out like a light when I finished my shower so I let you sleep. When you're done you can grab your gear and meet me in the restaurant for breakfast." John walked out of the room.

Mike continued laying there a moment thinking perhaps things will get better today. He hated not waking up beside his wife, hearing his children scurry about the house and even missed their runt of a dog always jumping on the bed licking his face each morning. How could he possibly take these things for granted again?

"Sit down rookie and order some breakfast. We need to be rolling soon."

Mike sat down while he stretched and yawned. "It's too early for breakfast."

John gave a hard squint for a moment and strongly suggested, "Better order anyway. I don't know when we will stop and eat again." Mike nodded and ordered.

John finished his breakfast and was sipping on his second cup of coffee. Then in a childlike manner he apologetically expressed to Mike, "Sorry about the little burst of anger last night, rookie."

John took another sip of his coffee, “It’s a touchy subject these days. Next week will be the ten year anniversary of the accident and I tend to get a little cranky this time of year.”

Puzzled, Mike asked, “What accident are you speaking about, John? I don't know anything about it.”

“Never mind for now, we need to be going, I'll tell you later.”

The sun was on the way up as John and Mike where putting their gear away in the truck. John walked around the tractor and trailer with the cheater bar in hand as he bumped the tires and checked the tension on the chains. Meanwhile, Mike raised the hood to check the engine and other parts of the tractor preparing for the day ahead. Finding a chain loose John called Mike over showing him the loose chain and handed the cheater bar to Mike.

“Let's see if you can tighten this up.”

Mike loosened the chain binder, grabbed another link on the chain and proceeded to pull down on the binder with the cheater bar. Watching closely John waited until the last moment when the binder was about to slip and grabbed Mike out of the way before the bar could hit him on the head.

“Now you know the wrong way to tighten the binder and since you almost took the top of your head off I believe you'll remember this. Let me show you how to do it without hurting yourself.”

Mike watched as John put the bar over the binder handle, stood to the side of the binder and pulled it down until it locked.

Mike explained to John, “I never tightened a chain on a load before. I didn't know.”

John gazed at Mike with an understanding smile, “I know that’s why I’m here for you now.”

All they teach you in driving school is how to shift gears, back up, check equipment, do your log book plus know the rules the government feels is important to know. The rest will be up to people like me once you decide the type of truck you want to drive. You don't need to be a rocket scientist to drive a truck, but you better have an overabundance of common sense to survive. There are so many different loads to haul you must to be able to determine the best and safest way to haul each of them. You will come to realize you, as a driver, are the most responsible person on the face of the earth. No matter how the shipper loads your trailer. And you better believe me rookie the shipper will load it their way if you let them every time. But it's your ass will pay the cost if something goes wrong, not them. I will do my best to show you the right way to do this job. Always remember, you can learn just about anything you seek from a book and go to a school for just about anything you want to attempt to master. However, you cannot teach a person common sense. You either have it or you don’t. It’s as simple as that, rookie. Mike truly felt like a rookie at this moment.

John asked Mike if he was ready to drive for a living now. Mike nodded and got behind the steering wheel. He told John he’d never driven a conventional tractor before since they only had cab over tractors in school. John explained it wouldn't take long to get used to it. Mike sat back behind the wheel of the Pete and looked out the windshield at the long hood. There was so much space being blocked in front of him he was actually scared to move. He did not want to hit something or someone.

“How can I tell what's in front of me?”

John giggled a little at this too often asked question. “You will get the feel of it in time. Just pay attention to what was there before.”

Mike hesitantly put the truck in gear, then released the clutch. He was starting off on his new trucking career. It was a time he would remember for the rest of his life. Even though he didn't realize it at the moment it would become second nature to him. Once he was on the road he started to settle down a little. But he couldn't relax behind the wheel yet as this would come much later when he gained more confidence in himself and the truck.

"Driver, park your truck and bring your paper work inside." This came out over the loud speaker at the Georgia State Weigh Station in a very commanding manner.

"What do I do, John?"

"I suggest you do as the man says unless you want to spend some time in a Georgia jail."

Mike pulled the truck over in a parking spot and walked into the station with his permits. He stood there for a while at the counter until finally he heard a voice from up the stairwell.

"We can play this game all day. Or you can come up here and show me your permit, driver. I'm not coming down there!"

Mike walked up the stairs to the scale master. He presented the permit to him and patiently stood there. He suddenly felt very nervous as sweat started to cover his body.

The scale master scrutinized over the permit trying to find some little technical flaw in the writing of it. Not seeing anything he could use against the driver and sensing a new driver as well he decided to go a different route.

"Where's your log book, driver?"

Mike handed his log book over to the officer who took even more time looking it over. The officer handed him his log book and went back to watching his readings on the scale.

After a while the officer looked up and very sternly said, "Can I help you with something else, driver?"

Mike answered in an adolescent manner, "I'm waiting for you to tell me what to do."

The scale master made a sweeping motion with his hands and very roughly growled, "Just get the Hell out of here, driver."

Mike went back to the truck trembling. He climbed in and looked over at John who had a devilish smile on his face.

"Asshole's just as cheerful as ever I suppose."

Mike frowned and mumbled, "Uh huh."

For what it's worth rookie not all are like that, only a few. It's important you know how to deal with them. I don't know what their problem is and neither do the people who have to work with them. They seem to either hate their job or hate dealing with us, or both. The point is always be prepared for the unexpected when dealing with civil servants.

Mike nodded. It was another reason he might be starting off on a career he did not want. Time would tell he supposed. He considered if he had time he would have shared God's love with this person and perhaps made a difference in their life as He had in his. He decided a thoughtful prayer would have to suffice for now. He couldn't help but wonder though since his wife was also a state worker. Did she treat the public in such a manner? If so, then why? It was something he would discuss with her when he returned home, but more importantly how much he missed her at the moment.

Traffic was a little heavy through Spartanburg often called *Sparkle City* by truckers and also Charlotte often called *Queen City* by truckers as well. The really good part was no problems at the state weigh stations. Even though it was rush hour, Norfolk traffic was no more congested than usual. Perhaps it was the cooling promise of fall air. Or maybe the beauty of the region rich with history, but Mike could sense a comforting easiness as he drove though Virginia. They made it to the truck stop in Kings Dominion just before dark. Mike observed the obvious age of the truck stop and thought it was somewhat pleasant. It was also considerably farther north than he'd ever been in his life. So he was a little apprehensive about the mannerism of the local people and what it would mean to him.

“Let's get our gear and check into the motel,” said John.

Mike noticed this truck stop was somewhat more upscale compared to the one the night before with the motel actually inside the truck stop facility. He would learn later this was very common among full service truck stops in years past. Mike and John went to the room to stow their gear. Mike noticed the room was a little nicer than the one before and had a television as well. They stowed their gear and walked down to the restaurant for dinner. That's when the difference caught Mike’s attention full force. Mike ordered fried oysters on special for the night. When the waitress delivered them to the table he questioned why they were in the form of square patties. He was informed oysters in the area were always prepared in this manner. He cut into one which had such a foul smell he simply could not eat them. The waitress removed them with apologies. He ordered a hamburger steak. When he finally received his replacement meal it was very overcooked, dry and also appeared to have been premade instead of freshly prepared. He attempted to consume it the best he could, but was not very happy with it. After their meal they returned to the room, showered and settled in to watch a little TV. Mike thought about it for a while and asked John if he felt like telling about the accident he mentioned earlier.

John glanced toward the ceiling a moment, “Ten years ago next week was probably the worst day of my life.”

Hammer Lane and I were hauling steel rebar rods. We loaded in Birmingham going to Little Rock headed across US 82 in Mississippi. As usual we were hauling ass that night while I was running the front door. We were talking on the CB radios which were something new at the time and simply having fun riding along. Hammer hollered at me on the radio. He told me there was a strong odor of rubber burning. He wanted to know did I feel anything wrong since he didn't think there was a problem with his truck. I didn't feel anything either. So I just laughed it off. He told me it was getting stronger and maybe we should stop to check it out. I refused since I didn't believe it was a problem. We were only a few miles from the truck stop in Winona where we could inspect everything. At that moment I felt a vibration in the steering wheel. All of a sudden the driver's side steer tire blew out and the front end dropped sending me quickly off into the Mississippi woods in the pitch black night. Past this point is still a blur in my mind. I may never remember all of the details concerning the accident. The doctors say the trauma effect of the accident was to blame.

The next thing I remembered was waking up and seeing Hammer standing over me and what was left of my cab over White Road Commander. Strange, but I do remember thinking at the time of an old saying we had about cab over trucks. You're always the first one at the scene of the accident! I was thrown from the truck and lying on the ground and wedged between a tree, the fuel tank and left side of the truck. I was in a lot of pain and everything was blurry, but I can still see Hammer standing there with an empty fire extinguisher in his hand plus another empty lying on the ground beside me. I could smell smoke and I could see a little flame toward the back of the engine. Hammer was telling me help was on its way and not to worry yet I could see the concern on his face. We tried to get my right leg loose from under the tank, but couldn't quite get it out. The flame at the back of the motor started to get larger. Then I panicked and I begged Hammer to get his pistol just in case. I simply didn't want to burn alive under the truck. Hammer told me to hold on while promising he would get me out. I think I passed out for a while and came to when Hammer started shaking me. He told me he chained his trailer to the wreck and was about to try and pull it off enough to get me out. I stayed conscience the best I could when I felt the tank and truck start to move off of me. I guess it slipped and fell back against my leg as I heard and felt the bones breaking under the weight. It was then I passed out for good. The next thing I remembered was waking up just enough to realize I was on a stretcher. I noticed a cop put my friend Hammer in hand cuffs. I looked around and saw a firetruck putting out the flames on what was left of my truck.

I screamed out to Hammer, "What's going on here? Why are they arresting you?"

Then a paramedic came over and told another one, "He's come to, put him back out!"

That's when the lights went out until several days later when I awoke in the hospital. For a few days after I couldn't remember anything. I didn't know who I was or anything about the wreck. That was a scary feeling. Everyone telling me who I am, but I had not one memory of my life or anyone in it. John paused for a moment to reflect as Mike sat there trying to think of what he should say.

Then without thinking it out more clearly Mike blurted out, "I thought you said Hammer was a friend of yours. I've heard this story before while I was in driving school. They used it to demonstrate what a fool Hammer was. They said he should have waited for the rescue squad to get there instead of taking matters into his own hands. He almost cost you your life for God's sake. How can you defend someone who put you in so much danger?"

There was anger in John's eyes for a moment. Then he realized few people knew the truth about that night and to jump down this kid's throat would not help anyone at this point. He thought a minute instead pondering if one more knowing what happened would matter at this time. He decides to tell the truth.

"You have to understand there are things in this life which aren't what they appear to be. There is always the right and the wrong along with a thin gray line between the two where in most cases the truth will be."

Mike listened in disbelief at John's remembrance.

Hammer Lane Express

It was several days before I started to remember who and where I was. The first thing happened was the local sheriff kept coming in and taking statements on the accident and the involvement of Hammer. Then, which didn't seem too strange until later, the chief of the local volunteer fire department started to come by asking questions about that night. The more I started to remember it seems the more they questioned me. There were even times they would doubt what I told them. They'd say things such as, *are you sure it didn't happen this way*, and try to change my answers to what they wanted to hear. When I would ask about Hammer they would change the subject or just ignore my questions all together. I managed to call our company and when I asked about Hammer they would only say he has been fired. I should try to get over my injuries and get back to work as soon as I could. Don't worry about a thing and especially the man that's responsible for me being in the hospital. The more I tried to find out the more confusing it became for me. I still didn't have a crystal clear memory of that night, but the one thing I did know is there was no way Hammer could be responsible for the wreck. He most certainly was not responsible for my being in the hospital. He saved my life so far as I was concerned. With my leg in the shape it was, the months of rehab it would take to walk again, I should get help and get to the bottom of this. My next move was hiring an attorney to get answers for my questions.

Mike sat and listened to John's story intently. He had a hard time believing what he was hearing. Why would the authorities charge and hold Hammer if he didn't have something to do with it? Why would they try to get John to change his story? It just made no sense to him. How could this be?

“So you got a lawyer. Did he get the answers you wanted?”

“Not at first,” reflected John, “he hit some of the same road blocks I did. He soon realized things simply didn’t add up and information was slow and hard to get.” John stretched back.

Until he found Hammer was still in jail and was allowed no visitors other than his court appointed lawyer. He had a conversation with Hammer's attorney. He found out his attorney had very little experience with this type of case and really didn't know which way to go with it. With my permission they decided to work together to try and get to the heart of the matter. That's when they found they were in the middle of a major cover up concerning the events of the accident.

When Hammer went to move his truck to hook up to the wreckage a State Trooper came up and helped him get situated. Hammer's tractor was partially in the road so the Trooper set up in the middle of the highway to keep traffic from hitting him. Hammer began pulling and when he thought he moved the wreck enough to get me out he climbed down and went back to drag me from the wreckage. The Trooper stayed on the road directing traffic. Hammer pulled me back up to the side of the highway and that's when my tractor flamed up and started burning. Hammer went back to his truck and unhooked the chain and started to move his truck to the side. As he was moving his truck the volunteer fire truck came up too fast and swerved to miss him, hitting the Trooper's car. That sent the car flying where it struck and killed the Trooper. The little volunteer fire department was under investigation and was in danger of being disbanded plus facing more law suits. So with no witnesses to the incident other than the volunteers, they decided to do some damage control. One thing you must learn is the fact as a truck driver in this country you are considered a second class citizen with no rights to speak of and very dispensable. In short Hammer was charged with blocking emergency vehicles along with manslaughter since they felt he caused the accident with the Trooper. If not for one of the volunteers confessing the truth Hammer would have grown old in state prison.

Mike and John both sat there in silence for a long time. John perhaps reflecting on what was and mostly what could have been. Mike letting what he just heard set in while just shaking his head in disbelief. Mike had always been of the opinion law enforcement was beyond reproach and could always be trusted. The one thing he would learn as a driver is the only thing separating him from them was the gun, badge and uniform. They are still men and women who have the same feelings, instincts, along with the will to survive as everyone else on earth. And as such can make the same mistakes.

"So what happened to the people trying to frame Hammer?"

John straightened up in his chair. "Well, basically nothing at all."

The fact was they still had Hammer and was not giving him up easily. It took some back room talking by the lawyers along with the Judge, but in the end they decided it was best for all to walk away and not discuss the matter anymore. Hammer had to sign some papers stating he would not discuss the case. Nor would he seek recourse against anyone involved in the cover up. I guess that's why all you ever heard about the wreck was what was reported since no one else involved could say anything to correct it.

On that note John and Mike agreed it was time to go to sleep. Mike lay there and went over the story again and again thinking can it be so easy to get into so much trouble out here? He thought about it some more and realized not only was this the loneliest time in his life and not only did he miss his family more than ever, but after hearing the story he now felt the most vulnerable, helpless and frightened since he was a young child. More and more he was thinking have I made a bad mistake here? He asked God for His guidance as he did every day. Life seemed a lot simpler a few months ago. Sure times were tough and money as always was very tight since there always seemed to be a special need by one of the children. Though he never regretted helping with his brother and sister's education he often wished he had the same chance to attend college. Would life be better for his family if he had? Would he have married and have the wife he has now? Would he have the children he has now? Was it wrong to think of his life in this manner? He prayed to God for clarity. Father, please show me the path. Sleep took over before he could achieve an answer.

"You want home fries or gravy with your order?"

"Believe I'd rather have grits, please," answered Mike.

"Sorry, we don't have grits yet. But we're working on getting them, babe."

John chuckled, "Get the home fries rookie. They're sort of like fried tators down home."

"Okay," agreed Mike thinking there he goes again with that rookie crap.

The waitress then remarked, "Down home. Where's home for you?" looking at Mike.

"Alabama!" The pride was prominent in his voice.

"Oh, I love that new country singing group from there called *ALABAMA*. The singer called Randy, he's so cute! And I love the song *The Closer You Get*. Do you happen to know them?"

"No ma'am," replied Mike, "believe they're from Fort Payne. I'm from Montgomery and besides I'm not into country music anyway. An old rocker you know."

John broke in, "That will change in time rookie, if you hang with driving very long. Country music and trucking have always gone hand in hand."

Mike shook his head and blurted out, "Don't believe so. I can't stand all that twanging crap. It's mostly because I had to listen to it at home as a kid. Mom and Dad were big fans and didn't like me listening to rock." Mike shook his head again.

Mike then exclaimed, "So you may as well give up on me and country music. Not going to happen!"

"Sure kid, we'll see in time."

That's when the waitress brought their meal. She placed everything neatly and stood a second smiling at Mike. Then she sweetly remarked, "You say Alabama, huh?"

"Yes ma'am."

"Come back to see me, baby. I just love the southern accent and the quaint mannerism you have."

"Yes ma'am," as Mike began to feel his face turn red.

After finishing breakfast and settling up with the truck stop and motel they went to the truck and prepared to meet the day. John drove out that morning knowing full well the traffic around Washington, DC would be more than Mike should have to deal with at this time. Going around the loop Mike stared in amazement at the traffic and at the manner, in which they drove remarking several times, "These people are crazy as blazes! Don't they see this truck sitting here?"

John just smiled knowing some things in this trucking life will never change. Washington, DC traffic was one of the constants in life. They were both glad to see Gaithersburg and get to the job site to unload the steel plates. Mike was amazed when he learned the steel plates were to be used on site to fabricate a new city water tower. After unloading they went to a small corner store to call in for the next load. With no load yet, John decided to go the truck stop in Jessup to sit and wait where they could get a motel room if needed. It was late afternoon when the page came over the intercom from their dispatch. John went to the fuel desk and answered the page. Dispatch gave him a load for the next morning at the steel mill in Baltimore going to Beaumont. Mike was a little excited after learning they would be going to Texas. There was something almost mystical to him about the Lone Star State. Being a big western movie and TV fan it was one of the places he always wanted to go and visit.

"Best move on up, rookie," said John as they sat in line at the steel mill. Mike reluctantly started the engine, released the brakes and moved up another truck length. He shut it back down and looked over at John.

"This doesn't make any sense at all. Why can't we sit here until they're ready for us to load?"

John just sighed and explained, "Because if we don't move up the drivers behind us will do one of two things. They will either try to go around us or walk up here wanting to know why we aren't moving up. Now which would make you the angriest after sitting here for about six hours?"

Mike leaned back in the seat and sighed as well. "The steel mill does pay us for this time waiting, don't they?" Perhaps Mike anticipated the answer to his question.

"You're joking, right? It's just part of the job."

It was two and a half hours later when they finally loaded and tied down. Both men were tired and ready for a long rest although it was not to happen tonight. John drove out of town back across Interstate 66 to Interstate 81. He then proceeded south to Raphine, Virginia where they stopped to eat a late dinner.

"Are we getting a room here tonight?"

John shook his head. "Not tonight, rookie."

It's after midnight and we have to be in Beaumont in a little over thirty hours. This means we have to run tonight and maybe we can get some rest tomorrow night. Interstate 81's not too bad from here to Interstate 40 just outside of Knoxville. So you'll drive to there and I'll nap over in the passenger seat just in case. If everything goes alright I'll drive from Knoxville.

Mike scratched his head. "Neither you nor I have the hours left to drive tonight." Mike's face showed the shock he felt.

"We can't do that!" It would be against the hours of service rules, John!"

John slowly sat his coffee cup down on the table and leaned over toward Mike as if to whisper a secret. "If you're going to make it in this trucking life you better make a decision now."

Are you going to drive and work 100 percent by the DOT rules and constantly go from job to job because you keep getting fired for late freight? Which in turn you only wish to make the money you want or need and only if someone else will hire you. Or are you going to learn how to make the rules work for you and do what you must to survive? Think about it. Today at the mill could have been and in time will be you all alone with no one there to help you load, tie down and tarp. Then after all is said and done you will still have to be in Beaumont in the same time frame with no one to help you drive. What will you do then?

Mike thought about it a while, "I don't like having to do this at all, John."

John, understandingly replied, "No one does."

It would be nice to work a job same as any other worker, drive your shift and go home and sleep with your wife. Then get up and do it all again tomorrow. But this is the real world where the attitude is drivers are a dime a dozen and expendable. If the customer has a problem getting his load on time then fire the driver and keep the customer. If the driver gets caught doing what you told him to do or lose his job then fire the driver and keep the government out of your pocket. There's always another driver in line waiting to take his place, at least it appears to be the attitude of today's trucking companies. We all surely hope one day it will change for the better, but the sad truth is the powers that be like it as it is.

Take all that free time today waiting to get loaded plus the time it took to tie the load down and tarp it which we don't get paid for. Multiply those by the untold number of loads were loaded today across this nation and consider how much it holds down the cost of goods in this country. This in turn holds down inflation. Don't think for one minute the government doesn't know and count on this. Keep John Q. Public happy and they'll keep voting you back into office. I'm sure there will be an accident one day will change some things. I'm also sure the only one to pay the price will be the poor fool driver who was trying to make a living for his family and not the ones who are really responsible. The shippers, the receivers, the trucking companies and most of all the government allowing them to keep getting away with it!

Mike sat there in deep thought for a moment and smiled at John, “Then let's get out of here, we've killed enough time.”

Mike started out down through Virginia in the dark of night. It was his first time driving a truck at night outside of driving school and soon realized it was a totally different world after midnight. He was easing along at the 55 mph speed limit as trucks were passing him by at an alarming rate. One truck went by and called out to him on the CB radio.

“Hey large car Peterbilt, what's the problem? Is your fuel filter stopped up?”

Puzzled, Mike asked, “What's a large car, John?”

“It's a truck, often a conventional with a high horsepower engine, but mostly not governed to a specific slower speed.”

Usually they are not governed down to a low speed like most company trucks are. Company trucks governed to say 65 or 70 are considered big trucks. Trucks that run more say into triple digits are considered large cars. In other words, a big truck runs as fast as he can. A large car runs as fast as he wants!

“What I'm trying to tell you is he's talking to you, rookie!”

Mike picked up the microphone, “I don't think so. Why, do you see something wrong?”

“You're running so slowly, that's what's wrong!”

"I'm doing the speed limit. Why is everyone else going so fast?"

John tapped Mike's shoulder, "You can pick up the pace if you want. Just jump in behind one and go!"

Mike hammered down and caught up to the truck, "Okay, I'm behind you now so you better keep me out of trouble!"

"Sure thing Peter car, I've got the front door. What's your handle?"

Mike looked over at John, "I don't have a CB handle. What do you think it should be?"

"That's entirely up to you. You're the only one who knows your interest, background, hobbies and such, rookie."

Mike thought about it for a moment. Just what could he use? It had to be something reflecting his life or interest. He was drawing a blank, but had to come up with something quick. Under pressure he turned to the One he always had. God, please help me. My mind is a blank. What should it be, dear Lord? Then as always he got his answer.

"Hey Large Car Pete, what do they call you on the radio?"

Mike suddenly picked up the microphone and for the first time in his life proudly answered, "They call me Rookie, driver!"

Hammer Lane Express

Chapter Two

Life has no speed limit

"I'm sorry, Mike is not here. May I take a message?" his wife asked the operator. The telephone operator asked Mike would he like to leave a message. "Please have him call this number when he returns," then gave his wife the number to the pay phone he was using.

Less than a minute later his wife called him back. It was a system they worked out prior to him going on the road. He would make a person to person collect call to his home phone asking for himself. When his wife answered she was to tell the operator he was not there and ask if she may take a message. Mike would then give the number of the pay phone he was using which in turn she would dial and call back direct. This would be the cheapest long distance rate. Even then long distance calls were so expensive they would only do this on Wednesdays. He would call on Friday if he was going to be out for the weekend. If he was he would call on Sunday evening. It was also a system numerous drivers used which could make life on Wednesday nights around the truck stops very interesting.

"How are the kids doing?

"They are getting more hardheaded each day same as their daddy. When are you coming home?"

Mike could sense a strong concern in her voice. "Don't know yet. We pick up Monday here in Houston for Pittsburgh. So I don't know when we'll be there. I don't know where we will go from Pittsburg. In fact, I'm not sure about anything right now. Only I miss you and the kids. I love you so much!"

With a long sigh, "I miss and love you too, honey. Are you sure this is what you want to do for a job? I don't like being alone all the time and having to deal with everything by myself."

Mike wished he could reach through the phone and just hold her for a minute and reassure her they made the right decision for the family. But how could he convince her when he was not convinced it was the right decision with all that happened so far?

"If we're going to save enough money for a down payment to build a house and put back to help the kids go to college I'm going to have to do something other than put tires on cars and trucks. You know how we have struggled even with you working and we have already invested so much time and money into this. I really can't see where it would be smart to quit now."

She knew he was right, but still wished things were different. She may not realize now, it does take a very special woman to be a truck driver's wife. Mike was thankful to have one of the best.

After talking with his wife and kids for a short time Mike wasn't sure if it actually helped or made things a little worse. He was glad to hear their voices, but now missed them more than before. He just wanted to go home and stop playing this game called TRUCKING and all the pain it was causing at the moment. He took a minute and looked around the truck stop at all the people going about their lives and wondered if any of them felt like he did at this moment. Or have they learned how to cope or maybe just had nothing better to do. He felt he was a decent man with a few faults and worked hard to correct them.

Hammer Lane Express

All around him was a totally different world until a week ago he never knew existed. He recalled Friday night as John and he were trying to sleep at the motel when it seemed about every five minutes or so an ambulance would go by. Or a police car screamed past. Or gunshots would ring out. Then there was the occasional knock on the door which John told him to ignore.

"Wouldn't be anyone you or I know."

Then Saturday morning while walking over to the truck stop restaurant and getting stopped twice by prostitutes he knew existed, yet had never seen nor met before in his life. He somehow thought if a woman was to decide to do such a thing she would dress and conduct herself to be highly desirable. However, this turned out not to be the case. Even if he were single he wouldn't want to talk to these women, surely not make love to them. Yes, it was a world until now he never knew existed. What else would he experience? Only God knew.

The worst for Mike was Sunday morning. As long as Mike could remember, with the exception of events making it impossible, he was always in Church at least for services if not for Sunday School as well. Now here it is Sunday morning in Houston at a rat hole of a truck stop in a dilapidated motel room with no Church in site.

"Is there a Church nearby we can attend?" he asked John.

When John turned away from the television, Mike thought he may need to run, "A what, Rookie?"

"A Church, John!" answered Mike.

"What for, are you dying or something? And I don't know where you get this *we* at!"

Mike was shocked. He never had a situation such as this. He thought Lord please help me! "I just thought it would be nice if we could attend a nearby Church for services."

Mike added, "I've always gone to Church every Sunday for as long as I can remember."

"Well you just do that, but leave me out of it. I have no use for any man's Church!"

"John, the Church belongs to no man. It belongs to God!"

"Oh really, then why do all have one thing in common? There's someone always walking around taking up money. If there were a God what would he need with money?"

Mike shook his head in disbelief. He knew all too well he was not a minister and he could never answer these questions on his own. He thought God you have given me a mountain and a mountain of a man at that since John was a very tall and large person.

"John, the money is a love offering to help people in need and to spread the word of God. We do this out of our love for God and those around us."

"Again, what does God need with money? If there is someone in need why doesn't he help them Himself?"

"He does! Through us! That's what being a Christian is about, helping others in need instead of thinking only of you!"

"Good since right now I need another beer. So you take your book and read it to yourself. You can call it your Church over in the corner there. Cause we aren't going anywhere around here and that includes you!"

"John, I'm not afraid to go anywhere because I know God is always with me."

"Then you just go ahead and walk up that street. When the hoodlum pulls his knife out and asks for your wallet you can tell him that. Then you can ask your God where he is as you lay on the ground with your guts around your boots!"

Mike knew it was surely going to be a work in progress. He also knew this was no place to go walking alone. Perhaps God has put this before him to temper his mettle. He had so much to consider. He was sacrificing along with his family so dearly, but the one thing he simply could never do is sacrifice God. Nothing was more important to him. He would have to make a decision when he got home. For now he would need to seek guidance in God's word. He spent the remainder of the evening in solitude with his Bible.

Supper at the restaurant was very somber as well. Neither wishing to start another deep discussion when at the moment both needed the other somewhat for protection in an uncertain area. After taking turns to shower and preparing for bed sleep came quickly. Mike pondered his existence and purpose for being where he was at this time. This in turn led to an interesting dream of family and home. Perhaps in this was God's answer for him. Then possibly the answer was for Mike to find for himself and not to be given by God until needed. The only thing for sure was Mike had many difficult decisions to make and soon.

John told Mike it was time to go as he got up from the table and stood there a second while he finished what was left of his coffee. Mike nodded and got up as well. Then they paid their ticket and started walking to the truck.

John nervously remarked, "Stay close and keep your eyes peeled. I don't like walking across this lot in the dark, but we need to get ahead of this traffic."

Mike did as he was asked though it didn't need to be said. Some things are instinctive such as wanting to live another day!

They got to the truck and John gave Mike instructions. "Let's go over it real well and hope everything's still here."

Mike started walking around the truck and bumping the tires. He looked under the trailer to inspect the brakes.

Mike suddenly jumped back as if snake bit and yelled, "What in the blazes!"

John ran toward Mike with the cheater bar in hand.

"What's wrong? What is it?"

Mike and John stood there in shock as a hobo came from under the rear of the trailer dragging an old beat up bicycle and a couple of bags.

John went off on him, "What the Hell are you doing under there? Get your sorry ass out here! That's all we need, take off and run over your dumb ass and have to fill out all that paper work for nothing! Which is exactly what you are you stupid asshole, nothing!"

Mike stood there in shock as the hobo responded, "I just needed a place to stay warm and dry for the night. I knew you and him were in the motel since I saw you come in Friday afternoon. And I knew you wouldn't be going anywhere till today. I just didn't know you'd be leaving so early. Besides, if you check you'll see nothing is missing on your rig. I kept the ones who steal away from it."

John thought about it a moment then pulled his billfold out and gave the man a ten dollar bill. "Thanks. Now get breakfast on us."

The man left pushing his bike down the road toward the corner store.

Mike stood there a moment still in shock. "That was a nice thing you did for him. He looked as if he hadn't eaten in days."

"Yep and I guess you noticed he didn't go toward the restaurant, but rather to the convenience store. The wine and beer is more important to him than food."

Then John glanced at Mike, "Guess you learned why it's important to walk around your truck before leaving now."

Mike nervously answered, "No doubt about that!" They climbed in to leave and load for Pittsburgh.

John pulled out of the truck stop and headed for the pipe yard. It had been a very stressful weekend. Perhaps the coming week would be a little better for both. Soon they were there.

"This is nothing more than a mud hole!" as Mike got out.

Hammer Lane Express

Mike was trying hard to find a solid piece of ground to walk on at the pipe yard where they were now parked.

"Welcome to Houston, Rookie. There are only two seasons here, wet and muddy, dry and dusty. Guess which one it is now?"

They laid the four by four timbers down on the bed of the trailer getting ready to load the steel pipe they were to take to Pittsburgh. After they set up and were waiting for the crew to come load John felt the over whelming pain of nature calling.

"I'm going to the portable toilet over there. If they come to load us be sure they start about three feet back from the headboard. We are loading forty foot pipe and we have a forty five foot trailer. It'll be too heavy on the drive if they start any further forward and too heavy on the trailer tandem if they go any further back."

Mike nodded and John walked off. As luck would have it the loading crew which consisted of two Mexican Americans on a large Petibone bend in the middle fork lift came up with the first layer of pipe. They started loading the pipe all the way up against the headboard. Mike walked over and informed them to move the pipe back about three feet.

The driver looked at Mike and smiled a big smile, "No hablo ingles," in Spanish.

They sat the pipe down on the trailer and proceeded to get another layer of pipe leaving the first layer all the way to the headboard. They returned with the second layer and were about to put it down in the same manner when John returned. Mike told John what happened.

"You don't know how to talk Tex-Mex in Houston, Rookie?"

"I can't speak anything but English. Most people would have their doubt that is true."

John walked around to the truck side box and reached in and got the cheater bar. Then he walked back over to Mike.

"Tex-Mex is one of the easiest languages in the world to learn. Pay attention."

When the crew was lining up to set the pipe down John walked over to the fork lift and told the driver, "Amigo, I need you to move this and the pipe you just sat down back about three feet."

The driver as before with Mike smiled widely and started speaking in Spanish and turned away to start setting the pipe down as before. John again stopped the driver and asked once more to move the pipe back three feet.

Again the driver smiled widely, "No hablo ingles." He then proceeded to load the pipe the same as the layer before.

John reared back with the cheater bar and came down so hard on the fork lift the driver jumped up from the seat.

John told the driver, "I want this damn pipe moved back three feet from the head board and I want it done NOW! Or the next thing I hit will be your head, compendia amigo?"

The driver looked at him saying, "Yes sir! About three feet you say."

"Sí mi buen amigo," replied John.

Mike laughed, "I guess they speak English after all."

"No, you just learned how to speak Tex-Mex in Houston."

When you ask them something do they answer you with a large almost childlike smile as they speak Spanish? Or do they look at you with concern and a blank stare as they speak Spanish. If they are smiling and or grinning they know English well enough to know what you are saying. If not they probably know little or no English and don't understand what you want. Don't get me wrong, I have nothing against Mexican Americans. In fact I have several Mexican American friends which are the reasons I know about this. After years of being played a fool by a few stupid Texans they just can't resist getting one over in retaliation. However, consider this. The majority of drivers who pick up pipe here all speak English only. Now do you really think the owner or supervisor is going to put two people on a lift to load these trucks that do not speak or understand English? Of course not since how else is the job going to be done efficiently? That's why they just can't help but smile the same as anyone pulling a practical joke on someone else. But in a situation such as this we don't have the time or money to play diplomats! I don't and never have tried to play them for a fool and I sure as Hell won't put up with the same from them when we have to get to Pittsburgh as soon as possible. It's just a sad part of life and the vicious cycle of stupid continues.

After loading and chaining down the load of pipe Mike and John pulled back onto the road and headed toward the Keystone State. Having looked forward so much to seeing Texas Mike was glad to see it in his mirrors now. Perhaps he would come back again sometime, but for now he needed to let the experience soak in for a while.

Mike drove across Interstate 10 through Baton Rouge and then Interstate 12 to Interstate 59 North into Mississippi. Then he drove through Mississippi to Meridian where they stopped at the Queen City truck stop to eat dinner. Mike looked at the menu.

"Finally, food I recognize. Give me the cubed steak, green fried tomatoes, black eyed peas, turnip greens with corn bread, banana pudding for dessert with sweet tea."

John agreed, "Make those two orders, the same."

"It's not Bama, but it is nice here," Mike remarked as they waited on their food.

John nodded his head. "The Magnolia's pretty nice. There are some very good people here and some extremely good friends. In fact, there comes one now!" as John smiled.

Just then an older lady with light red almost pink hair came up to the table and patted John on the back.

"How have you been doing, Big John?"

John turned around, stood up and hugged the lady.

"Why, you sure are a sight for sore eyes, Maggie." She sat down beside John. John introduced her to Mike, then Mike to her.

"What's your CB code name, Mike?"

"They call me Rookie, ma'am."

"That's nice, Rookie. Never understood why it's so important for everyone to have one, but guess it doesn't hurt anything. Well John, guess Wednesday will be a sad day again this year, huh?"

John looked down as if to say a prayer for a moment.

"Yeah, it sure will be, Maggie."

Mike spoke up, "John told me about his accident ten years ago Wednesday. He said he still gets a little ill at this time."

Maggie looked a little puzzled for a moment, "That's right! It was about ten years ago this week you had your accident. I suppose I just forgot since Hammer was killed. Sorry John, I surely didn't mean to belittle your accident."

Mike looked totally confused.

Then John explained, "That's okay, Maggie. Mike probably did think you were talking about my wreck. I don't believe he knew you were talking about Hammer's. But you're right, Maggie. Very odd but both accidents occurred on the same day of the year. Guess it's just another reason I tend to get so moody this time of year."

Maggie smiled, "I still miss him. He sure was always good to me. Pulled me out of a tight several times and there'll never be another like him."

"Rookie here tells me the truck driving school he went to considered him to be a legend."

"A legend, I'd never have guessed it. Although he did have a knack for being at the wrong place at the right time I suppose. Whatever happened to that poor tanker driver in the wreck? How's he doing or do you know, John?"

John shifted his head to one side, “Don't know.”

I would go by to see him now and then at the hospital. We got along well at first mostly I guess because I had a time after my accident where I had no memory of anything same as he was going through with his memory. It's a scary feeling and having someone who's gone through the same experience has to help I would think. That's the biggest reason I kept going by. Plus I would like to know exactly what happened that day. You can understand why I have my doubts when it comes to relying on government investigators' explanations on the details of the accident. Seemed like the last few times I went by he was more withdrawn and just didn't want to talk to me. Then the last time I went by he was gone. He felt the hospital had done all they could for him and he needed to get back to some kind of life outside of a medical facility. They said he still had no memory of his life and with no family to speak of didn’t have anyone to try and work with him. His burn wounds were healed as much as possible with all the skin grafts so they could no longer hold him. They had no idea where he went.

Maggie, John and Mike sat in silence for a long time. Perhaps each was considering the story and where it actually would lead.

Then Maggie asked, “I was told he really looked pretty awful much like the man from the horror movie was burned so badly. Is that true?”

“Don't know, I guess he could have. But the last time I saw him he was still bandaged up. All you could see was his eyes and he had a little hole to speak through which made it hard to understand him. I haven't seen him since and never knew where he lived to try to find him anyhow. Don't guess it matters, it won't bring Hammer back.”

With that Maggie got up from the table.

“Got to get back to work, take care and don't be a stranger, John, you too, Rookie.” Maggie walked back into the fuel desk.

Mike finished his meal and sat there a while thinking.

"I wonder about something."

"What's that, Rookie?"

"I never thought about it before, but guess the tanker driver would have to stand out a little in a crowd. Especially if he's still driving a truck, wouldn't you say?"

John thought a moment. "I guess he would, but as far as him driving a truck again with all his problems would be a little too tough for most people to overcome. So I wouldn't expect to see him out here again or at least I haven't seen anyone I thought could be him."

"Guess you're right. He'd probably never drive a car again, let alone a truck." With that they got up, paid their bill and left.

Mike thought as they went through Birmingham only ninety miles from home and I can't go by. It just didn't seem fair. "I could stop and get my gear, call my wife to come get me and stop this insanity," he blurted out loud before he realized it. He glanced back at the sleeper and John was still asleep.

I know she wouldn't mind at all and probably would get a speeding ticket trying to get here quickly as she could. They'd take me back at the tire store. He didn't like to brag, but he was very good at what he did. Perhaps he was too good since they overlooked him for a promotion. Instead giving it to what he considered to be a slacker type worker who got where he did from the sweat of others and not his own. But there were others to consider here carrying far more weight in his decision. His children! There were two strong boys and a beautiful little girl who deserved a better life. One he could not provide selling and mounting tires for a living. And with no more education than he had his choices were limited.

The seemingly godless people he was coming in contact with now were something he never really considered. Sure he knew there were a large number of lost souls in the world, but until now were only a thought. Not only was he among the many, but stuck in a truck with one! From John's own account he had many close calls with death and should know more so than anyone God's hand was involved. Yet for some unknown reason he still denied His existence! He thought maybe God had another purpose for him at this time. If he should try another occupation then God would point him in the right direction. For now he would continue until such time God revealed His plan to him. So when he saw the signs for Interstate 65 coming up he didn't hesitate. He turned his signals on then moved over to the left to get onto Interstate 65 North going to Nashville. We'll give it some more time and maybe things will get better.

John took over driving in Cullman and Mike crawled into the sleeper for a long deserved nap. It took a while for him to go to sleep with the truck moving, but once he got used to it he was deep in dreams. Things were quiet on the CB radio and John was lost in thought as they rode toward Nashville. After going through Nashville he continued toward Louisville where he got onto Interstate 71 North headed for Cincinnati. He figured if everything went alright they'd be in Pittsburgh by noon. Just another day in the life of a trucker he thought.

But this trucking life was changing rapidly and before long he knew there may need to be a decision made. Accept the new rules and life politicians were in deep discussion about or find another line of work. It was a hot topic of discussion among the older drivers. There was a strong consensus deregulation of the trucking industry had placed trucking on a slippery slope to disaster. It appeared the only winners in the long run would be the businesses dependent on trucks. Already rates were on the decline and shippers were demanding more from trucking for the same money and in most cases less money. It was the main reason John sold his truck and had given up being an owner/operator and taking this job as a company driver after making the statement years ago he would never drive for a company again.

And there was another problem seemed to be adding fuel to the fire. With deregulation being implemented there was a sudden rise in new trucking companies since obtaining operation authority was becoming easier. With more trucking companies meant less freight and more competition for what little freight there was. It also meant more accidents and higher insurance rates. Plus there was stronger competition for drivers with a clean driving record which made for cheaper insurance and less hassle from the government. It was leading a push for more new trained drivers who by default would probably have little or no bad history on their driving record. This opened up an influx of new driving schools to train these drivers.

Until recently there were few driving schools in the nation. Most drivers either started out in a family business their parents or other family members owned and were taught by family to drive. Others worked at freight terminals loading or unloading trucks then moving to spotting trailers on dock doors. Eventually they would be given a chance to ride and then partner drive until they had enough experience to satisfy the insurance company. This was changing and the results were not very good. Anyone who had enough money and time could skip the hard dues of working their way up to driving by going to a driving school. This meant there was a new breed of driver taking up where the older more experienced driver was leaving. The danger in this was unmistakable, yet the need for them was reason enough to overlook the coming danger. Yes, before long John knew he would have a tough decision to make. He felt as though the day was rapidly approaching. He really enjoyed his job and hated to see so many changes. Time would tell he supposed.

Hammer Lane Express

There are very few pleasant surprises in trucking. Upon arrival at the oil field pipe preparation plant they were offered a reload of ready pipe to Broken Arrow. Mary, the owner, personally handled the arrangements and told John everything was set up for them. They were there only about an hour and left for Oklahoma.

"That was a stroke of luck getting loaded where we unloaded, don't you think, John?"

"You got that right. It doesn't happen very often with a flatbed, I can tell you for sure."

"Where is Broken Arrow anyway?"

John smiled, "Ever been to Tulsa before kid?"

"You know I've never been out of Alabama before getting in this truck with you."

"It's just outside of Tulsa and in a day or two you will be able to say you've been there."

The sun was setting low as they were easing across Ohio. Traffic was light and Mike was looking around at the scenery. There were a few rolling hills and then another flat valley. It was pretty farm country and he thought at the moment how lucky he was to be able to see it.

John gave instructions to Mike. "Don't forget when you get to Indy get on the Loop and go south west toward Louisville. Then take Interstate 65 South to exit 99 and get off then turn left into the truck stop on the right. Got that Rookie?" Mike nodded his head yes.

The old Stop 99 Service Center was slowly showing its age. It had been a popular stop among drivers for many years. They walked over to the motel and John registered a room for them. They then went and stowed their gear in the room. Fairly nice, it would do for the night. Then off to the restaurant for dinner. They were enjoying their meals as each remarked how tasty their food was. Mike happened to look up and noticed a man sitting at the bar and suddenly smiled with anticipation. Just then the man glanced over toward Mike and abruptly looked away as if to hide.

Mike reached over and tapped John's hand. "There's my friend Bob, sitting at the bar!"

John turned around to look. "Where is he?"

Mike went to point at the man, but he was no longer there. Mike got up and stood so he could get a better look, but still could not see him. He walked over to where he was sitting and noticed some money laid by his ticket where a half empty cup of coffee lay steaming. He walked through the truck stop then to the front entrance to the drivers' room, the convenience store, also the restroom, but no sign of the man. He went back to the table where John waited. He sat down looking totally confused.

"Where did he go?" asked John.

"Don't have a clue."

I know it was him as it couldn't have been anyone else. He does stick out in a crowd. That's why I asked about the tanker driver down in Meridian the other night when the lady said what she did about his appearance. I never asked Bob what happened to him, but evidently he was burned badly at some time in his life. And he never mentioned it to me either. Guess that's why we got along so well since I always treated him as if he were no different than anyone else.

John listened then remarked, "I don't think he's the tanker driver because his first name was James and knowing how badly he was hurt I don't see him driving a truck again. However, I would still like to meet your friend."

Confused, Mike shook his head. "I can't understand it since I know he saw me sitting here and I don't know why he would leave in such a hurry." Mike stood and looked again.

"Maybe I was just mistaken, could have been someone else."

They got up and paid their check and went back to the room. Tomorrow would be a long day. Mike took his shower first then sat and watched a little TV while John showered. After a short time they both decided it was time to sleep. Before long John was snoring in deep slumber. But Mike laid there and kept thinking about the man he saw at the bar. He was almost positive it was Bob and could not understand why he would leave so suddenly without at least talking to him. All he could think happened was Bob didn't see or recognize him and left in a hurry for some unknown reason. It made for an interesting dream.

"How long will it take to fix it?" the concern was strong in John's voice.

The service manager at the Caterpillar repair shop answered, "About two hours once we get started. We should have a man on it in about four or five hours."

"Well, I guess we have no choice in the matter. We can't run it skipping as bad as it does."

John looked over at Mike, "At least we made it to the Cat house here in Saint Louis before the injector went completely out. We won't be here long enough for a motel room so guess we'll have to settle for their waiting room."

They walked upstairs to the drivers waiting area and settled in for the wait. TV didn't work very well, but they did have some fresh coffee to drink.

Mike glanced over at John, "How much do you know about the wreck with Hammer Lane, where he was killed?"

John thought a second, "I guess this is the first time ever I was about to let the day go by and not remember the anniversary of my wreck. And Hammer's as well! If you hadn't mentioned it I may have forgotten." John leaned back in his chair.

"There's not a lot I know. Only what I was told by the Tennessee Sheriff at the hospital where the tanker driver was."

The best the Sheriff could determine they were running down US Highway 421 toward Mountain City from Bristol, a very hilly and curvy road they recommend trucks not use. Hammer's Kenworth was the lead truck and the driver in the International cab over fuel tanker was behind him a little way. It's not clear if they were running together. They think Hammer was probably going way too fast when he came around the curve where a Chevy van was broken down. He tried to miss it, but clipped the left corner of the van and rolled over going length ways off the bluff and into the nine hundred foot deep gorge below. It caught fire on the way down exploding at the bottom. The tanker driver evidently was warned by radio by the first driver since he started braking before rounding the curve. He still couldn't stop in time before hitting the van full force which was all the way across the road after being clipped by the first truck. Instead of hitting the van and surely killing the people inside the tanker driver went to the right and up the hill missing the van then turning over spilling fuel as he went. The tanker driver was thrown out and covered in fuel which soon caught fire. The people in the van went to his aid, but without a fire extinguisher all they could do was take a blanket and try to cover him to put out the fire. We really didn't think he would make it to the hospital, let alone survive. He must really have a strong will to live after all the pain he was going through.

Mike asked, "Did they try to do anything for Hammer?"

"I asked the same question of the Sheriff."

He said by the time his deputy got to the scene the Kenworth was well involved and he could not find where the driver had been thrown free or left the truck and informed the rescue squad perhaps they should contact forestry. There may need a bulldozer to control the fire to keep it from spreading into something much larger. Being so deep in the gorge the best they could do was circle it with the dozer while wetting it down and letting it burn out. The fire was so hot there were no usable remains for the coroner to determine identity. Only the tag registry was used to confirm the driver as Hammer.

Mike shivered as a chill went through him. "I guess there are many terrible ways to leave this life, but this has to be one of the worst I can think of."

"Yeah, it was tough for Mary to take. She's the one who had the cops stop and inform me so I could go to the scene because I was in Knoxville unloading at the time. When the authorities called the company to let them know about their truck they didn't know it was his wife who answered the phone!"

Mike's face took on a look of shock. "What do you mean his wife? I never knew he was married! And why would they be talking to his wife when they called the company?"

"Rookie, who do you think owns this company? You met her when you hired on. Mary Bryant, Hammer's wife."

It was a small struggling outfit at the time. Think we had about six company trucks and four lease trucks, mostly buddies of Hammer's. I happened to be one of the lease trucks at the time. Hammer was driving one of his own trucks and Mary was doing the dispatching plus all the office work. Yes, when they called the company to inform them about their truck it was Hammer's wife they were talking to.

"Sorry, I had no idea. I never actually met her. At least I didn't see a lady there when I hired in. You mean in fact I'm working for Hammer Lane?"

"No kid, you're working for his wife, Mary. She is a very smart lady and the heart and soul running this company."

She took the insurance money from his accident expanding the business into what it is today, one of the fastest growing trucking companies in Alabama. As I told you before in this trucking life things aren't always as they appear to be.

Just then the door opened and a mechanic said, "Are you guys in the Dixie Carriers Pete?"

John got up, "Yeah is it ready?"

"Not yet, just thought I'd let you know I'd be on it as soon as I come off break."

John just nodded and sat back down and looked over at Mike, "We better close our eyes now and try to get some rest. We are going to have to roll when they get done."

Having gotten out of the shop late they had to run nonstop to Broken Arrow. After unloading they went to the Union 76 truck stop in Tulsa where they spent the day waiting on another load. Mike remarked how Oklahoma was not what he thought it would be. He said he didn't expect it to be so hilly and open. John said some of it is a little flat, but most is like what he was seeing around Tulsa. He also said it was an oil boom state in years past, but was changing fast with more oil coming from overseas now. Most oil fields here and in Texas were being slowly shut down since the cost of pumping the oil out was making it hard to compete with the low cost of Middle Eastern oil. It would take a major price increase of oil or complete depletion of the oil fields in the Middle East to justify restarting some of the oil fields which all the experts agreed would never happen or at least not for another sixty years or more. Besides, by the year 2000 we'd be using something other than oil anyway, probably alcohol or electricity or something else new. Yes, it was a changing world especially in Oklahoma and Texas. Didn't know how people here would survive. It was almost sad as during the Great Depression when dust storms carried away the top soil.

Late afternoon they got the call from dispatch to go to Duke to load for Salt Lake City. They decided to go down to Duke and stay until morning and get loaded early. John napped over the wheel and Mike took the sleeper as he would drive later.

They were loading at a wallboard plant where John was having a very heated discussion with the fork lift driver.

"I don't care how most drivers let you load this crap! You will load it the way I want it or you will take the damn stuff off my trailer and we'll charge you for a truck not used."

The fork lift driver continued to argue, "I'm telling you that all the drivers want it loaded heavy to the rear and that's the way I'm going to load it."

John then yelled, "The Hell you are!"

Most of the trailers you have been loading here are ten foot two inch spread axles which are allowed up to forty thousand pounds on the trailer tandem. My trailer is a dual tandem and only allowed thirty four thousand pounds. Plus in Oklahoma they only weigh the gross weight of the truck and trailer to make sure it's not over eighty thousand pounds and not the axle weights as other states do. In other words, you will load this trailer as I say or take the damn stuff off!

After getting the supervisor involved they finally agreed to load it as John wanted. "Do you see what I meant when I said the shipper will load it their way if you let them? You and I will be the only ones who will pay the cost if we get caught."

John was still mad even miles up the road at the broker who the company got the load from. It turned out after getting loaded and covering the load and they went to the shipping office to get the bill of lading, only then did John discover they had a stop off in Lincoln. This made the trip considerably longer and made the load pay even less per mile than before. John said it was a trick some underhanded brokers would use. Especially to get a load moved they knew would be hard to get covered. They would list the load from one location directly to another for a certain rate or amount of money and when you figure the miles for the money it would look good. The broker would know the load had a stop off somewhere else making the load pay more because of the miles involved. But they would purposely leave out the information there was a stop off thereby making the load appear to pay more per mile than it actually did.

The reason John was mad is he was not paid by the mile, but rather a percentage of the gross money the load paid. This meant he would have to drive more miles and work harder having to uncover the load for the stop off and then recover the load to go on to Salt Lake. All of this extra work was out of the goodness of his heart he guessed. He couldn't quite figure out whether he was angrier at himself for getting cheated by a dishonest broker since each time he swore it would never happen again. Or the really sad thing was the owner would put a little something extra in his pay envelope even though it was not her fault and the broker gets away with another one. Yes, there are people out there who are waiting for you to let your guard down and play you like a fine tuned fiddle, he thought. He'd try to stop it from happening again the best he could.

"Go straight up Interstate 35 to Kansas City and then take Interstate 29 North on up to Iowa. After you cross into Iowa take the exit for Highway 2 and go west. We'll go into Nebraska and then up to Lincoln. I'm going to take a nap so wake me up when we get into Nebraska. Did you get all of that, Rookie?"

"Think I did. If I forget, I'll wake you up."

Mike did as John told him and when he came into Iowa it was already dark. He got off the Interstate onto highway 2 and went west as John said. The exit clover leafed around and then back under the Interstate. As he started west he noticed a large sign stating *Legal Vehicles over 8 feet wide Prohibited 2 Miles Ahead*. He was not sure what it meant. How wide was the truck and trailer he was driving? He wasn't sure. Then he saw another sign stating the same thing, *Legal Vehicles over 8 Feet Wide Prohibited 1 Mile Ahead* and again he was not sure, but there was nowhere to stop and find out. He called for John to wake up, but no luck, John was sound asleep. Then there was another sign, *Legal Vehicles over 8 Feet Wide Prohibited 1000 Feet* and then he went around a curve to the left. He came out of the curve and his heart dropped. It was a narrow steel structured bridge with one lane each direction and the total width of the bridge was only 16 feet. Too late, he had nowhere to stop and definitely nowhere to turn around. There was also traffic coming at him on the bridge. So he looked straight ahead and said a quick prayer as he hoped for the best. A little over half way he heard something go *WHAM* on the passenger side of the truck, but did not dare take his eyes off the road to look over. He'd wait until he got off the bridge before worrying about anything else. As he came off of the bridge he was now in Nebraska and John was climbing out of the sleeper.

John sat down in the passenger seat wiping his eyes, "Got the mirror, huh?"

"Don't know, afraid to look over there right now. I don't think I can move my head right now anyhow."

"Was it a narrow bridge or what?"

"Narrow was not exactly what I would call that bridge, more like ridiculous!"

"Just pull over at the wide spot up there and we'll check and see how bad it is."

They pulled over and looked at the mirror. It was knocked back at an angle with the door, but was not broken or damaged.

"You're very lucky this time Rookie, most of the time it would at least crack or break the glass out and have to be replaced. Let's reset it and I'll take over."

Mike sat on the passenger side and wondered if he would ever stop shaking. If so, how long would it take him to get over it?

"Guess we'll have to report it and I'll have a chargeable accident on my record now."

"What are you talking about, Rookie?"

"The mirror,"

"I don't know anything about a mirror," as John winked and nodded his head.

"What would have happened if I had broken the mirror or brace or something?"

"We would have gone to a truck stop or parts store and bought another one then replaced it ourselves, wouldn't we?"

"Guess we would have done that!"

"You just go ahead and clear you head in the cool air, Rookie. Soon as I can shake the cob webs out of my head I will drive on into Lincoln. You can lie back in the sleeper if you want and just try to settle down some if you can. When I get there I'll just nap over the wheel until they show up."

The stop off went well since they were not sure if the customer would be open or receive it on Saturday. John told Mike they would go on toward Salt Lake and probably stop in Cheyenne for the night. John drove across Nebraska as Mike looked around. Mostly flat farm land and plenty of it. Mike thought how nice it was to see all the crops nearing harvest and how good it all looked. It had been a long day and they both where glad to see the Little America truck stop in Cheyenne coming up. They parked the truck and went to the motel to register for a room and settled in, then walked across to the restaurant for dinner. They both remarked on how good the food was and how reasonable the prices were. They decided they would stop at the Little America on the west end of Wyoming the next evening. After their meal they went back to the room to relax before bed.

"Let's see what's on TV," as Mike turned it on.

Hammer Lane Express

John stretched out on his bed with the pillows piled up so he could see the television.

Mike flipped the dial through the channels and soon found there was nothing on worth watching. "See anything on you like?"

"No, nothing piques my interest on the thing."

Mike turned it off and started sipping on a cup of coffee he brought back with him from the restaurant. He thought a minute and decided now would be a good time to ask John about the boss lady. "I was a little curious about something."

"What's that, kid?"

"I've not meet the boss lady, Mary. What kind of woman is she? I mean what's she like?"

John took on an odd smile, "Sure Rookie, I'll tell you the story of Hammer and Mary."

"She's nothing like Hammer was, I can tell you that much right now. In fact I'd say she's about the opposite from Hammer a person can be. I remember the first chance encounter these two happened upon. And let me tell you it was not a good thing!"

Hammer started his dedicated run out of the roofing shingle house in Birmingham to Dallas and back. He pulled into the yard in Birmingham and was waiting to load along with about twenty other trucks. It was a little tight at the docks as usual and the drivers were getting very impatient. There was a green Western Star conventional just finished loading. By procedure the driver should have pulled off the dock and pulled around back to tarp and strap down. Hammer would be the next truck to get on the dock to load. This would be soon as the truck moved off the dock. But instead of moving off the dock there was a slender woman with long fire engine red hair who climbed up on the trailer and started to roll the tarps out over the shingles. This infuriated Hammer so he walked over to the woman to complain.

"Where is your husband at, ma'am?" asked Hammer.

"Don't have one, driver."

Already agitated he decided to question her once more. "Then where is your boyfriend?"

"Don't have one of those either, driver," as she continued to work.

Hammer, tired of playing this game asked, "Then where's your Dad?"

She stopped what she was doing, "My Dad left us when I was a child. Now what the Hell do you want?"

Hammer blasted out, "I'm just trying to find out who's driving this damn truck so I can get them to move it the Hell around back so I can get on the dock and get loaded!"

She looked him up and down then remarked, "You're looking at the driver, the owner, the banker, the mechanic, the dispatcher and the boss. So mister, just exactly which one would you like to kick your ass for you right now?"

The one thing Hammer was probably most guilty of is he was about as close to a male chauvinist pig as you could get. I mean the whole women are to stay at home, have babies, clean house, cook meals, lie down and have sex when you, the man, wanted and most of all never be allowed to drive a truck. He believed it would be the end of trucking as we know it. And not only was this one driving a truck which was yet to be seen, but also was threatening to kick his ass. Which he thought she may could do since that's about how high she could get anyhow.

Mary, she was a text book example of a women's liberation movement poster child and damn proud of it! Fire and water would be an understatement when trying to compare them. After the loading dock foreman talked to her she agreed to go around back to finish securing her load.

But before she left she looked at Hammer and told him, "This ain't over, pig face. I'll see you out there somewhere and we'll finish it then!"

"Sure thing sweets, till next time!" as Hammer patted his butt.

It was about an hour later when I got to the shingle house and saw Hammer around back tying down. He asked if I saw a green Star leaving as I came in on the interstate which I hadn't.

Then he proceeded to tell me what happened, "I tell you one damn thing, Big John. That witch will live a long, lonely life, cause ain't anyone going to marry or even live with her. Except maybe one of them lesbian type girls which may be her problem, she probably likes girls you know."

"Now Rookie, I'd seen Hammer get worked up over a woman before, but this one was different. She really got under his skin and it bothered me since I had no idea which way this would go. Maybe they would never meet again. After all it is a big world out there."

Well, it is a big world out there. But there's not a lot of hiding room when you both are running the same dedicated run. That's what happened and neither one knew it at the time they met though it may not have made any difference. They were both on their way to Dallas as each had the weekend to get there since they loaded on Friday and didn't have to be there until Monday. Neither one had a home where they had to be so they each had a plan for the weekend. Hammer had friends in Dallas so he planned to go on and be there by late Saturday afternoon. Mary had family in Longview and planned to visit for the weekend. Neither one knew about the other or their plans.

Hammer pulled into the Union 76 truck stop in Greenwood before the Texas line at around two in the morning. He was getting sleepy and figured he'd nap till day light then go on to Dallas. He was riding around the parking lot when he spotted the green Western Star of Mary's. There was a parking spot to her left side open. He squared up and backed in besides her thinking they'd settle this in the morning when he got up. He had been riding for a long time and had to answer nature's call, but it was a long walk to the truck stop facilities. He was so tired he decided to just walk to the back of his trailer to the woods behind him and pee. He was relieving himself when he heard a strange noise toward the rear of Mary's trailer. He walked over to her trailer but couldn't quite make out the noise. It was a kind of a moaning, crying sound he'd never heard before. He looked under the trailer and there was Mary all huddled up in a fetal position like a little child. He could tell her clothes were torn and it appeared she was hurt and also bleeding. He calmly called out to her and she wouldn't answer.

He reached in to shake her arm to get her attention and as he did she screamed out, "NO, LEAVE ME ALONE, DON'T HIT ME ANYMORE!"

He calmly called to her, "What's wrong here, ma'am? Who hurt you?"

She then looked up and saw Hammer. She came scurrying out from under the trailer and grabbed hold of him. "Don't let him hurt me anymore! Keep him away from me!"

"What's going on here and just who is trying to hurt you?"

She pointed to the truck on her right side. "The man pulling the dry van there, he kept beating me and tried to rape me. I think he was going to kill me until you started to back in beside my truck. Then he ran off toward his truck."

"Let me get you to my truck and lock you in so I can go and call the cops and an ambulance for you."

"NO! I don't want anyone knowing about this! I just want to get back to my truck."

Hammer couldn't believe what he was hearing. "You can't let him get away with this! He has to pay for what he did or he will do it again to someone else."

"Please don't call the cops."

I don't want to be made a spectacle and relive this. I don't want to see the doubt in their eyes when I tell what happened and have even more shame to deal with. You just don't know how embarrassing it is to try and prove rape in a man's world.

Hammer didn't think it was right, but he knew she made a good point. Without a witness to what happened it would be her word against his in which case the cops and prosecutors would rather write it off than try to follow up and get a conviction.

Mary was a very strong and proud woman who had been forced at an early age to be self-reliant and also very mistrustful of men. What she didn't know was there is an animal out there even more dangerous to her than a man. This animal was not a beast with a sense of right or wrong and cared nothing about women's rights nor had any interest in anyone's political views be they liberal, conservative or libertarian. Heterosexual or homosexual were only words to him. Religious or atheist also had little to do with his world. As was anything else in life most human beings with any decency would hold dear. This animal is the human waste who just tried to rape her. He just happened to be driving a truck even though he could be a doctor or lawyer or have any other profession in life as this animal has done ever since the beginning of time. He had but one interest and she was it at the moment.

Hammer again pleaded with her to let him call the police, but to no avail. Just then he heard the air brakes on the rapist's trailer release. He asked her if she would be alright for a moment.

She hesitated for a second and then asked Hammer, "What are you going to do?"

"It's better if you don't know. Just tell me you will be alright for a little while. I promise I will not call the cops."

She said she would try.

Hammer went running up front as the driver started pulling out to leave. He ran up to the driver side and jumped up on the running board to get his attention. The driver rolled his window down and Hammer told him to stop.

"You've got something dragging under your trailer, driver. You may want to take a look at it since I don't know what it is."

The driver stopped and set his brakes then got out. Hammer and the rapist walked toward the back of the trailer. He noticed the man was quite a bit larger than he was, but Hammer was so angry the blind rage he was feeling would more than compensate for his lack in size. When they got to the rear of the trailer the driver bent over to look underneath. Just then Hammer drop kicked him in the face. The man let out a scream as he hit the ground quickly. When he started to get back up Hammer drop kicked him again then jumped on top of him hitting him in the face as hard and fast as he could. It wasn't long until the man was almost unconscious.

That's when Hammer started talking to him, "How's it feel big man to have someone beating the Hell out of you when you least expect it. You're luckier than the lady you just beat up though since I don't intend to rape you. Or at least I don't think I am," as he kicked him in the groin area which really got his attention.

The man started to cry and for a moment Hammer felt bad for what he was doing. Then he thought about Mary crying when he found her. The thought how she must have cried too as he was beating her which infuriated him even more. "What were you thinking and feeling when she started to cry? Where was your compassion as you were beating her and tearing her clothes off then kicking her senseless you damn piece of crap?" The man just rolled up in a fetal position like a child. Hammer thought, this is the second time tonight I've seen this only I don't care about this one!

It was then the police car came screaming up with the lights flashing. At first the driver tried to get up and run. But he was too hurt to move let alone run. Hammer just stood there over the man as he waited for the police to walk up. When they did they jumped on Hammer forcing him to the ground then handcuffed him. They helped the driver sit up and started to question him.

"What's going on here? Is this man trying to rob you or what?" as they pointed at Hammer who was standing.

The man just looked down and said nothing.

They looked at Hammer, "Why are you beating on this man? He's not even fighting back yet you were still hitting him!"

"Why don't you ask him again why I was on his ass?"

They asked the man again and he only looked down saying nothing. They asked the man if he wanted to press charges against Hammer for assault. He looked up and was about to speak when he glanced over toward Mary's truck and saw her standing there staring back at him. He put his head back down and shook his head no.

"Are you sure you don't want to file charges against this man? He's going to jail for the night and can't hurt you anymore."

The man glanced back over at Mary again who was still watching intently and again shook his head no. The cops then put Hammer in the car. They asked the man if he wanted an ambulance. He said no he just wanted to leave which they let him do.

The next morning Hammer was released from jail and caught a cab back to the truck stop. Mary's truck was gone and Hammer couldn't help wondering if she was okay. He got in his truck and left heading toward Dallas stopping at every truck stop and rest area he came to making sure she didn't stop somewhere needing medical help. He went all the way to Dallas and didn't see her anywhere. He could only hope she was alright.

"They told a story similar to this one in the driving school only they said Hammer was on drugs and beat another driver senseless. And most likely would have killed him if the cops hadn't stopped him, all of this over a parking spot!"

"I've heard so many different versions about this incident I can't keep them all straight. But rest assured I told you the true story as told by the only ones who matter, Hammer and Mary."

"Since now you know the story I suppose you can understand why neither one would speak up to change what has been told."

"I guess you're right," as Mike slowly nodded his head.

John grinned at Mike, "As I told you before, things in this trucking life are not always as they appear to be. Life has no speed limit so you better hold on tightly and be ready to adjust to whatever it may throw at you kid."

"Yeah, I can see that all too well now. I never imagined life in a truck could be so unpredictable."

"You have to be ready for whatever could be lying just around the next corner out here. I think I'll go ahead and take my shower. You can sit around and watch TV if you like or go take a little walk around Wyoming."

"Think I will go walk around and see some of the sites around here. I'll be back a little later."

Mike went outside in the cooling air of fall. It was almost cool enough for a jacket as he wandered across the truck stop parking lot. He went into the restaurant and refilled his coffee. He thought about calling home but since it was Saturday he decided to wait and call Sunday since funds for long distance calls were short. After paying for his coffee he walked back outside and noticed the huge mountain behind the truck stop. He decided to walk around the back and see what was there.

It was a very clear night and the stars seemed brighter than he ever remembered. Everything seemed vast as he realized the mountain was way further away than he thought. The silence was immense among so much beauty. It was a moonless night but the stars seemed to light the sky as though it was a full moon. Then he noticed something strange. Slow at first but increasing each time it appeared. At first just a streak of light then nothing as it almost seemed like a distant thunder storm working up. But the coolness suggested there could be no thunderstorm especially with there being not one cloud in sight. Then again he witnessed a streak of light in the distance a little brighter than before. It was an odd light almost like a search light spreading across the skyline. He couldn't quite understand what he was seeing as his mind drifted to possibilities. Could God be attempting to get his attention through the Wyoming sky? He stood in awe admiring the light when all of a sudden there were more streaks running across the sky. Only now there were different colors to them. It almost appeared to be the colors of a rainbow. He began to think there may be something wrong as he never witnessed this site before. He stood in silence for a very long time taking it in and wondering should he run for cover.

"Is there anything more beautiful in this world?"

Mike jumped as another driver was standing beside him.

"Goodness driver, I didn't mean to scare you so."

Mike gathered himself and replied, "No driver, I was just deep in thought at this miracle and didn't notice you walk up."

"It's no miracle; it's the Northern Lights you see."

"The Northern Lights, I've heard of them but never really seen them before. What causes them and where do they come from?"

"What they are is a reflection of the sun on the polar icecaps. That's why they have the colors of the rainbow at times. There are times they light the sky almost as day light. No matter how many times I see them I am impressed. I feel I am closest to God each time."

Mike smiled, "Yes, my thoughts exactly as I watch them."

Mike stood for a few moments then turned back to the driver.

"This is so amazing," and then Mike realized there was no one there. He was all alone in all the beauty of the show. He looked around and could not see one soul anywhere near him.

Hammer Lane Express

CHAPTER THREE

WHEN LIFE AND TRUCKING COLLIDE

AS Mike drove across Wyoming he noticed the scenery appeared to be changing. The mostly gray hills and light green grassy plains where giving way to a totally new look. The hills were becoming mountains. It also appeared the light green grassy plains where becoming sparse and a mixture of brown to a dark tan and then almost black at times. The mountains where also taking on a majestic look of brown and red with some tan and almost a golden color. Some of the mountains appeared to have huge flat rocks which looked as though they were piled upon each other. It was a beautiful site and he was enjoying it thoroughly. He also noticed on occasion as he drove along something would move and catch his eye but he couldn't tell what it was. There it was again, but what was it? He couldn't just stare at the plains and drive as well. He had to keep his eyes on the road even though traffic was very light. There it was again, something moved, but what was it? He thought for a moment he must either be seeing things or losing his mind yet there it was again. *I know I saw something move!*

He was really getting concerned there may be something wrong with him. Then as he glanced over to the right at the plains he finally saw what had been catching his eye for so long, an almost mystical creature responsible for numerous poems, books and even songs.

"ANTELOPE!" exclaimed Mike. "There's so many antelope on both sides of Interstate 80 you could never count them, John!"

John glanced out from the sleeper, "Yep, guess there are. Wake me up when we get to the Little America." John lay back down and closed the sleeper curtain.

Yes, there were herds and herds of antelope scattered all over the plains. They could blend in so well with the grasses and mountains they were practically invisible to the naked eye. On occasion something would spook them. They would run a few feet and stop to see what startled them. It was only then you could see them since when they stopped they become invisible again. He thought how lucky he was to be able to experience this for free.

Little America Travel Center on the western end of Wyoming was quite a bit more upscale than the one on the eastern side of the state. It was at least twice the size and also appeared to be newer with many more items for tourist. There was also a larger driver's room. Oddly for a truck stop there was a waiting area with a full service bar for restaurant seating. The waiter escorted them to their table and gave them a menu. The table already had silverware wrapped in cloth napkins along with coffee cups turned upside down. The waiter came back and asked if they would care for an appetizer before dinner. John and Mike looked at each other confused.

Mike simply informed the waiter, "No thank you."

They looked the menu over and John mentioned, "I've never been here before. I'm already beginning to wonder if this is a truck stop or just what the Hell it is!"

Mike shook his head as he looked around the room.

"I've never been in a restaurant like this in my life let alone a truck stop. I believe it's a little out of my price range, too. I believe we made a mistake coming in here. There is nothing under ten bucks!" commented Mike who then chuckled.

"You got enough on you to eat here kid?"

"I may be able to afford the ten ninety nine hamburger meal if I leave off the cheese," replied Mike as they both laughed.

Once they ordered and received their meals John remarked on how good the food was.

Mike agreed with him, "This may be the best hamburger steak sandwich I ever had."

"Yeah, it is quite tasty. And I have to admit I could get used to this. However, I do feel just a little out of place with waiters and huge cloth napkins."

"Well, it's not like we will be here all that often," as Mike continued his meal.

After finishing their meals they paid their checks then left heading for Salt Lake City. Mike climbed into the sleeper and took a nap while John drove off into the western sky full of promise for travelers. Mike lay in the sleeper and contemplated on the events of the day. He couldn't get the beauty of the west from his mind. He could only compare it to an addictive narcotic you couldn't get enough of, try as you may. Even though the weather could make Wyoming unbearable at times you couldn't forget the fact one day it would clear up revealing the beauty once again. Before long Mike was in deep sleep.

John, while later driving in Utah, reached back into the sleeper and shook Mike, "Better get up, Rookie."

Mike sat up then pulled the curtain back sleepy eyed, "Why is that, John?"

John explained the unbelievable situation to Mike.

"Because I've been going down a very steep grade for several miles now and I don't know how much longer it goes. All I can see behind the trailer is smoke. I'm picking up speed fast, the brakes are gone!"

Mike shot out and got in the passenger seat then looked back behind them as he saw the brake smoke hazes rolling off the back of the trailer. He then remembered the conversation John and he had about the correct way to use the brakes going down a long grade. It was a heated topic among most drivers. Each one with their own way to do it without having problems with brake fade which is the point where the brake drums and brake shoes become so hot the brake shoes start to powder and act more like a lubricant meaning the vehicle gains speed instead of slowing down.

John was of the mindset the best thing to do was to use only the trailer brake hand valve leaving the tractor brakes fresh to stop the truck if the trailer brakes were to fail. As Mike had pointed out the problem is the tractor brakes are not sufficient to stop both parts at high speed or on a steep downgrade. He tried to convince John to use the foot brake thereby using both tractor and trailer brakes in a light manner and stab or apply lightly slowing the momentum and release a second or two then apply again keeping the brakes at an acceptable temperature while staying in a lower gear using compression from the engine to slow also.

To make the situation more understandable they were now up the proverbial creek without a paddle. All they could do was hold on for dear life. To make matters even worse when they got to the bottom of the grade there was a sharp left hand curve. At this point they both swore the truck went up on nine wheels while going through the turn! After they straightened up they were in downtown Salt Lake City. Plus the exit for the business they were to deliver was coming up and they still could not stop! They went by two more exits before the brakes cooled enough to slow down. They had to get off at another exit, turn around and go back.

John looked over at Mike apologetically, "You may have something with the stab braking deal, may try it next time."

Mike sat there and was speechless as he was still trying to get the feeling back in his butt. He couldn't remember praying as hard nor being as scared in his entire life. There was absolutely no way John could deny God's hand protecting them through the ordeal. They got off at their exit and found the customer.

"You can get back in the sleeper and I'll nap over the wheel until they come to work, Rookie."

Mike sat shaking from the event he just witnessed. There was no way the truck should still be upright! "No, think I'm going to walk around and get some feeling back for a while. You can get in the sleeper if you want. Besides, it may be a long while before I can sleep in the truck again, John."

Do you think there is no God now; being the only question he could think to ask John? Mike held back since it would appear he was being insensitive. He was sure John was as frightened as he. Mike walked around and looked at the area all the while thanking God he was able to walk upon this land rather than be scattered among the sand and stone in the curve on Interstate 80! It may have been a good time to speak with John about God's love after the event. However, perhaps John needed some time to let it sink in as well.

After unloading John and Mike went to the Salt Lake City Union 76 truck stop and registered for a motel room. Mike took their gear to the room as John called dispatch to check for any progress on another load. Mike unlocked the door to the room and stepped in to stow the gear. He looked around the room which was very small. It only had two twin beds, one chair, a closet and a small TV. He gazed a second and thought something is missing. Then he realized what it was. There was no shower or toilet! What kind of motel room is this he thought? He locked the door and went back to the restaurant to find John. He was sitting at a table sipping on some coffee as Mike sat down with him.

"You been here before?" asked Mike.

"Yeah, I've been here a time or two, why do you ask?"

"I went to the room and it doesn't have a shower or a toilet."

"It's down the hall, one toilet for all the rooms. We go to the fuel desk and show them our room key to get a shower."

"That sucks, not much of a room."

"We may not be here very long. We could possibly get a load this evening for tomorrow or wait and perhaps get a load sometime tomorrow. Don't worry, Rookie. Just sit back and enjoy the west today. Consider there's not much difference than what roaming cowboys lived with back in the old west."

They ordered lunch and were enjoying their food when the page came in for the Dixie Carriers driver. John went to answer the page leaving Mike at the table. When he came back John had a long hard look on his face.

"Mike, you need to call home."

"Why is that, John?"

"All I know is dispatch said you need to call home."

After Mike's wife called him back on the courtesy phone, Mike quickly got to the point. "What's wrong at home, honey? Dispatch said you called and there was an emergency."

"Crystal broke her arm today!"

"What happened to her arm, how did she break it?"

"You know the big oak tree in mom's backyard the boys have the makeshift club house in. Since the boys are in school guess she sneaked outside while mom was cleaning her house. She climbed up into the tree and fell out landing on her arm. She started crying and mom went running out and found her on the ground holding her right arm." Mike was listening intently.

Mom took her to the hospital and then called me. They took an x-ray and found a hair line crack in her right arm. She now has her little arm in a cast. She's doing alright for now and the doctor says it should heal with no problems, just keep her out of the tree! Anyway, she keeps calling for her daddy. She just won't stop crying for you. "So I wanted you to know and also see if you can try to calm her down," Susan pleaded.

Mike was a shocked and in total dismay. Of all the things he tried to foresee could happen and determine a path to deal with he never gave a second's thought to a problem at home. Probably because he was always able to respond quickly when an emergency arose and could be present at the drop of a hat. Now he is about two thousand miles away and has no idea when he will return. This was also his precious little girl and their miracle child. He thought all he can do now is try to comfort her on the phone while he prayed to God for his own comfort and thoughtful words for his little Crystal.

"Is she where I can talk to her?"

His wife put his daughter on the phone. "Daddy, I hurt my wing today. It hurts a lot, Daddy. Can you kiss it and make it better?"

Mike's throat swelled as the tears were ready to fall, "Princess, you know I love you and will do anything to make it feel better. But I'm a long way from you right now and I won't return home for a long while."

"But Daddy, it hurts badly. I need you to kiss it and make it stop. Why can't you come home now, Daddy?"

"Honey, I can't come home until my job is done. I'm trying to make more money for you and your brothers so we can have a bigger house to live in" as the tears started to well.

"But Daddy, I don't want a bigger house. I want you, Daddy!"

It was all Mike could do to try to hold his composure.

Crystal kept pleading with him to come home now.

He looked over at John. “My driving partner tells me we may get a load coming home tomorrow. Will that work, princess?”

“Will you be home tomorrow, Daddy?”

“Now honey, I can't be home that fast. You want me to be safe, don't you?”

“Yeah, but I want you to come home maybe the next day, Daddy. I'll be brave until then.”

Mike was about to lose it, but managed to say, “We'll see sweetheart, maybe day after tomorrow. You have to stay brave and don't let your Momma worry about you. Let her know you will be alright. Daddy loves you very much and will be home soon, okay?”

“Okay Daddy, I love you.”

“I love you too, honey,” Mike said as he hung up the phone. Mike looked over at John perhaps for some encouraging wisdom from his many years on the road.

“Does it ever get any easier?”

“Don't know, never been married. I certainly don’t have any kids. Perhaps it will just get a little different.”

Mike considered John’s little display of wisdom from over twenty years of trucking then looked John in the eye as he smiled then remarked, “Really! So this would be about all you have and have learned from over twenty years on the road to make sense of a senseless situation?”

“Yep, I suppose so.”

Mike simply shook his head slowly.

The dispatch called the next morning and they were on their way to Montana to pick up lumber going back to Birmingham. It seemed they would never get to the lumber yard, which is always the case when you have been away from home for a long time, especially if there’s a problem at home. As they were driving up Interstate 15 Mike couldn't believe how beautiful the scenery in

Idaho and Montana was with huge tall trees everywhere, majestic mountains with deep long beautiful valleys which seemed to go forever. He recalled another Alabama boy who fell in love with Montana, the mountains and valleys. They almost took his life when he fell from one of the mountains yet even with this Hank Williams Jr. still had a deep love and admiration for the land. Mike thought he heard or read somewhere with outstanding beauty will also lay immense danger. Guess this could be true, especially in the case of "Big Sky".

The trip back to Birmingham would be a long and hard one since they were loaded almost to the gross with lumber. The load was also tall and tarp covered which made it hard to pull in the wind as well. As they were going back Mike asked John why he never got married and had any kids.

Jokingly he made the remark, "You're not gay or something, are you?"

"No, I just never meet any women who could put up with trucking the way I do it."

Some guys want to be home every weekend and that's okay. Until now I've always owned the truck and had to keep rolling to make ends meet. Most women want to see you more often than every four or five weeks and surely wouldn't want to build a life with you on this basis. And if they did, well guess you'd have to wonder about that one, too. You being gone for weeks at a time can play right into a few women's plans, especially when they're cashing the paycheck, don't you think?

"I guess so, but what about now. You drive for someone else who takes care of the problems and expenses so why not settle down with a good woman?"

"Who are you trying to set me up with, Rookie?"

"I'm not, I was just curious is all. A man shouldn't live his whole life alone. Don't you want something that sort of looks like you some day?" John started to smile.

Mike quickly added, "I mean, don't you want to leave your mark on the world to carry on after you leave it?"

John laughed then said, "Well maybe, but I've been alone all this time. Don't see why I should be in a hurry to change now. I have some things I'm trying to get done so I can get out of this trucking life. When I get them done then maybe I'll seriously start looking around."

Mike happened to think of the story of Hammer and Mary's first meeting. He asked John what happened after the incident in Greenwood with the rapist and when or how Hammer and Mary met again.

John took a deep breath. "Actually they didn't for quite some time after that."

Mary took time off and lost her dedicated run before it even got started. Hammer ran the run for some time, but got tired of it then tried a run from Birmingham to Columbia, South Carolina and back. In fact let me tell you who he did run into before he saw Mary again.

Hammer was on his way back to Birmingham one night and stopped at the Big 'A' truck stop in Atlanta to take a nap. As usual the first few rows of the parking lot were full leaving the unpaved and downright mud hole back of the lot the only place to park. No one really liked to go back there since that's where most of the hookers and low life's did their business. He was in the back looking for a spot when something caught his eye. It was a cab over Mack pulling a dry van. As he looked closer it was the same as the rapist was driving though he didn't see the driver in the truck. There was a parking spot across from the Mack where he could watch the truck and see what happened. He got parked and began watching to see if it might be the same driver. He decided he wouldn't watch very long since he needed to get some sleep. It wasn't long until the driver came back. He unlocked the door and climbed inside. It was the same driver, the rapist from Greenwood. Hammer watched him for a time to see what he might do. Actually he hoped after the beating surely he wouldn't try it again. Deep down Hammer knew it probably didn't make any difference. And he was right.

There was a hooker working the back lot Hammer noticed before the driver came back to his truck. Hammer observed one of the security guards following her at a distance which probably meant she actually worked for him and he was keeping an eye out while she went truck to truck. Hammer saw the rapist notice the hooker walk behind one of the trucks. The driver eased out of his truck and went in behind her. Hammer opened his door and was about to climb out when he heard the first shot. He was on the ground and about to walk over to where he'd seen the driver walk in behind the hooker when he heard the second and last shot. He decided it was better to get back in the truck.

He sat there a while and after about twenty minutes a police car came up. Then a short while later an ambulance approached and parked. Shortly the paramedics came out with a stretcher holding a covered up body and placed it in the ambulance and left. After an hour he saw the hooker and the security guard walk by, but never saw the rapist again. He thought at the time guess that's one less thing to worry about now. Problem is there are plenty more to take his place someday. If only there was a way to determine who they were before their first victim. Hammer laid down and felt guilty he sensed a sick satisfaction this beast met his master, whatever it was!

Mike sat in silence for a moment. All life is precious. This is what he was taught, this is what he believed. No one should die until the hand of God comes to take them home. Until now this was not part of his ordinary everyday life. In a very short time he had been witness to and heard of deeds which simply could not have the fingerprints of his God upon them. This was beginning to totally complicate all he had come to believe.

“Darn, life can be hard sometimes!” exclaimed Mike.

"No, lack of respect for life and others can make it appear very hard. Not in all cases, but most people eventually receive exactly what they deserve. It just appears justice is a little slow coming sometimes, but come it will."

Mike was driving coming through Saint Louis while John lay napping in the sleeper berth. As Mike was driving he happened to look down at a car that'd been riding beside him for quite some time now.

"Darn, now this is about sick as I've ever seen!"

John rose up from the bed, "What's the matter, Rookie?"

"Come take a look at this idiot beside me."

John got up and leaned over to look out the window at the car, "Yes sir got you a good buddy trying to get your attention."

Mike, puzzled and confused had to know more, "A good buddy, what do you mean? I know good buddy is a term used for a friend on the CB radio, but what does it have to do with this?"

"The meaning of good buddy has changed since the early days. It means a homosexual or gay man or whatever else you want to call them."

Don't know why they do it, but they love to ride beside you and play with themselves. They will keep looking up at you to see if they are getting your attention. The best thing to do is pay them no attention at all. Sooner or later they will get bored and go to another truck and play their sick little game. Sometimes it can also be a con game or scam. Often it may be someone who is trying to bait you and see if you try to run them off the road or run into them. At which point they claim an accident occurred. Then make an attempt to get money from you or the company. With the image of trucking today plus the unwillingness of trucking companies to pursue court cases because of negative publicity they often will pay off any claim to stay off the news and out of the paper. Remember Rookie, things in this trucking life are not always what they appear to be. This is often one of those times.

"I sure would like to put him in the wall right now, but I see what you mean. John, when will we get to Birmingham?"

"About seven hours give or take. It may not seem like it, but it will go by quickly."

When Mike pulled into his driveway at home he just couldn't hold back the joy he felt. After being gone from home for almost three weeks he was ready for some down time. The first one out of the door was his wife followed by his two boys and little girl. They all came running to the pickup truck and grabbed him as he came out. No one could hold back their tears at the moment since it was so good for Mike to be home.

His daughter Crystal was holding up her little right arm with the cast, "Daddy, everyone has signed my cast except you. Sign it now Daddy, please!"

Mike pulled his pen out of his shirt pocket and signed her cast, *Love always to my little girl, Daddy*. Yes, it was so good to be home. After everything settled down Mike's wife started telling him all the things happened while he was gone and all the things needing his attention. Mike told her about all the things he had seen, leaving out some of the adventure he knew would worry her for now.

Then there was the one question that'd been on his mind for several days. "Did Bob call or come by at all while I was gone?"

"No, we haven't heard a word from him since you left, why?"

"Thought I saw him in Whiteland, Indiana one day, but I'm not sure. It might have been someone else. Maybe he'll call while I'm home. He should be curious about how I'm doing you would think. After all, he's the one made it possible."

"Yes and right now I'm not sure if it's a good thing or not!"

Mike stood and shook his head slowly, "What in the world has Bob so occupied he couldn't call, must be very important?"

Trucking is no different than any other job when it comes to home time. There's never enough it seems. Mike could have sworn he had just gotten home when dispatch called with a new load for them to pick up. Even though he'd been home for three days it didn't seem like it. Mike's wife was already back at her job with the state, but still he would like to stay home some more. He had to go back to work and attempt to do better for his family. When he pulled onto the yard John was already in the truck and had the engine running to warm it up. Mike stowed his gear and parked his pickup in the parking lot.

John hurried him into the truck. "We've got to go over to the shingle house and pick up a load of roofing for Florida."

"Florida? I wondered when we would get to go to Florida!"

John just frowned, "It was all came up for today so I had no choice but take it."

Mike asked, "What's wrong with going to Florida?"

John explained loads payed good going to Florida, but there was very little came out of there. What did wouldn't do any more than pay for the fuel. Really cheap freight state. But this was part of the game. You had to take the good with the bad sometimes. It could be an interesting break from the routine though. And it would give Mike an opportunity to witness driving a truck in a heavily populated area.

They stopped in Ozark, Alabama at Chisholm's truck stop for dinner. It was an old truck stop and had been there for years.

"Probably out live us all," John remarked.

The food was good, priced reasonable and they enjoyed it.

"More coffee?" asked the waitress.

"Sure," replied John.

"I believe she's got a thing for you, John."

John sort of blushed, “Give it up kid, it ain't happening. Especially with a waitress who is only looking for a bigger tip. Once I leave she'll do the same with the next fool.”

“Now John, you need to lighten up and enjoy life.” Mike also added, “You should stop being so negative. She may be the one you need but you'll never know if you don't try.”

“You really think so, huh?”

“Sure do, why?”

“Watch this kid,” as John waved to get the attention of the waitress.

“Hey sweetheart, come here a second.”

The waitress came over and John smiled sweetly at her, “How would you like to go out this weekend?”

“Now, why would you want to ask me out? You don't know me and I don't know you.”

“I will never get to know you if we don't do something outside of this restaurant.”

“They have a rule here, we can't date the customers. Sorry, no can do driver.”

“That's okay, you see I was only trying to show the kid here how misleading waitresses in truck stops are.” She popped him on the head and walked off.

Mike smiled, “Maybe I have a little more to learn about life out here.”

There’s one thing you need to keep in mind out here. When you're in a truck out there about everything in this world such as truck stops, waitresses, hookers, cops, weigh stations and just about anything and everyone only look at you as one thing, an unlimited source of revenue. The rest of the world looks at you as a nuisance, who would love to eliminate trucks if possible.

Mike smiled and nodded his head in agreement. Already he sensed there was a big difference in the manner most people acted around him as a truck driver. Sad, shouldn’t be this way.

The trip down to Tampa was going well so Mike stopped in Belleview at Grandma's Kitchen to get a cup of coffee while John slept. When he got parked he noticed an old station wagon car in the corner of the truck stop with several children in the back and a man and woman sitting in the front. While he was starting to get out the man came walking up to the truck. He had a cast on his left arm that went just below his shoulder all the way to and including his hand. It had several impressive looking pins sticking out of it which made it look even worse. Mike rolled down the window and the man climbed up laying his whole bad arm on the window seal.

The man began telling his story, "Driver, I'm a construction worker and I was working in Orlando when I fell off the building busting up my arm and wrist. I'm trying to get my family back to Texas and could use a little gas money."

Mike looked over at all the kids along with the man's wife, pulled out his billfold and handed him a twenty dollar bill. "God bless you. Hope you get home alright and get healed up soon."

The man simply told Mike, "Thanks," and went to his car.

Mike had never been to Tampa before. Orlando was the furthest he'd ever been when they took the kids to Disneyworld one year. After they unloaded they went back to the 76 truck stop to wait for a load. They went into the restaurant and sat down to eat lunch. John explained drivers called Tampa, Cigar City after the Tampa Nugget Cigar Company based there. Mike thought this was funny. They called Orlando, Mickey Mouse and Miami was Little Cuba and just about every large town had a CB nickname for it. It was late afternoon when dispatch called and told them they may as well come on out since there was nothing down there for tomorrow. They started back from Tampa and on the way John wanted to stop in Belleview at Grandma's Kitchen for dinner. The sun was almost set for the night.

John got parked and was waiting for Mike to get out of the sleeper when there was a knock on the door. John rolled the window down and a man said, “I'm a construction worker and was on a job in Tampa when I fell off the building......”

Mike looked out the sleeper and noticed it was the same man as the night before only he had the cast on his right arm this time. The man recognized Mike and immediately stepped down then took off running back to his car, got in and left.

John made the statement, “Now that was strange! He didn't even finish his story.”

“You mean lie!” said Mike. “That darn idiot was here this morning. I gave him twenty dollars to help get his family back home to Texas.”

John laughed, “I know. I wasn't asleep when you did it, I heard every word. That's why I wanted to stop back in here this evening and show you one of the oldest scams around.”

Mike was fuming mad, “If you knew it was a scam why didn't you stop me from giving him money?”

“I figured you'd give him a dollar or at the most a five. I had no idea you'd give him a twenty since I could not see what you were doing anyway or I would have stopped you. I'll give you your money back, but you still learned a valuable lesson.”

“No I appreciate it, but I made the mistake. I'll pay the price. It was my mistake for trusting people maybe I shouldn’t.”

It was just breaking daylight when they pulled onto the home terminal yard in Birmingham. John glanced over at Mike, “Think I'm going to take a quick shower. Then we'll be ready to go if something comes up.”

“Think I will too. It may make me feel a little better.”

After their showers they climbed in Mike's little pick up and went to a small local restaurant for breakfast.

"Why did you decide to drive a truck for a living, Rookie?"

"Well, the job I had at the tire store was getting me nowhere fast and my wife and I have been trying to get up enough money to make a down payment on a home for years."

We just couldn't seem to do it on what she earned with the state and what I earned at the tire store plus trying to raise the kids. Now I've been putting tires on trucks and cars for years, but never knew what driving a truck paid or involved until I meet Bob. He was a customer I meet a few years back and became friends with over time. I invited him to the house one time and he fell in love with my family. He knew what my wife and I were trying to get done so Bob started to talk to us about driving a truck. He is an owner/operator, but told me even though driving your own rig was the best way in his opinion, at first it would be better to drive for someone else and gamble with their money rather than ours. He told me about a state operated truck driving school in north Alabama. We researched it and found it cost only a fraction of the privately owned schools. But there was a long waiting list to get in it and you were not guaranteed to pass once you were. The course would take six weeks along with the fact I would need to stay there during the week since it would be too far to drive every day. We could come up with the tuition, but the expenses up there and here at home would be more than we could afford. Money was too tight and no bank would loan us the money. We just didn't see how we could swing it so it was only a dream.

Bob is the one who said make up your minds it's what you want and make no mistake about it, be very sure. If it's what you want I'll loan you whatever you need to get it done. My wife and I didn't want to involve Bob as we thought long and hard about it. However in the end we took Bob up on his offer and the rest is history.

John nodded his head slowly, "Sounds like a good friend who really cares." Mike nodded in agreement with John.

Then John commented, “That's a rare commodity these days when most people are only out for number one.”

“Yeah, I know! That in itself is quite puzzling to us because we haven't heard a word from him for quite some time.”

The last contact we had was the weekend after I graduated from truck driving school and I was to go to work here the next week. He seemed to be more proud of my graduating than I was. He just couldn't stop smiling and laughing. You would have thought I was his son or something the way he was acting. “And no, I'm not in case you were wondering,” quickly added Mike.

“Why don’t you just call him?”

“He doesn’t have a phone, that’s why. In fact, he has no where he calls home for that matter.”

He’s not leased to a company and only has Bob’s Trucking on the door of his truck. However, Dallas is the city on the door. Bob said it’s only a post office box he uses. It’s almost as if he doesn’t want anyone contacting him for any reason. I guess you could say we are the only family he considers having. He does have a bass boat though. He bought it about a year ago and he keeps it at my house.

“That has to be about the strangest thing I ever heard of. Are you sure you can trust him, especially around the children?”

“John, I trust him with my life. I can’t explain it, I just do.”

“Okay, we better get back and see what they have for us.”

They got up, payed their checks and went to Mike’s pickup when John said, “Hope they have something good for us.”

Mike asked, “Where do you think we will go?”

“Hard to say, could be anywhere. It’s a big world out there.”

“Guess we'll take the Dallas load. You got anything out there at the moment?” asked John.

“Not at the moment, John.” The dispatcher glanced at John.

"I should come up with something later if you want to call back. By the way you are going to be there tomorrow aren't you?" asked the dispatcher.

"As far as I know we will. That is unless we have problems getting loaded at the steel mill," John replied. "Better go get in line before it gets any later, Mike."

Loading at the steel mill went as expected. There were a few trucks in front of them waiting to load, but not as bad as usual. While they were in line an old friend of John's came up to the truck. As they all stood outside to talk John introduced him to Mike, "This is Gravedigger and this is Rookie, Bill," as they were getting acquainted. "Bill here is one of my oldest friends, Rookie. We go back to the old days when he and I along with Hammer plus a lot of others were company drivers for the outfit here in Birmingham I told you about."

Mike said "Glad to meet you. How in the world were you able to put up with John for so long, Gravedigger?"

"Easy," said Bill, "I was always in a different truck than he was and could get away from him whenever I wanted to. Now my question to you is how do you put up with him when you have to stay in the same truck with him?" They all chuckled heartily.

"Now you see why I like him so much. You just simply can't pull anything over on him, Rookie. He has a comeback for anything you throw at him since he's just simply too quick for you!"

Just then Mike thought he was beginning to understand a little about drivers and their friendships. They only see each other once in a while and can become so close out here. Even now he would have a hard time trying to explain it since it was not like working with someone on a daily basis and seeing them more than your own family. No, this was different and hard to explain without living it. The only thing may come close to compare would be soldiers in a war depending on each other for their lives and form a strong bond will last for the rest of time itself and then some.

"Kid, you were asking about Hammer. This man could probably tell you more about him than anyone else since he grew up with him!"

"Is that right, Bill?"

"Well, I guess so. I guess I know about as much as you could."

You see Hammer was adopted from a foster home as a child. I think he was around six or so when his new family moved to our neighborhood. He hadn't been with them long and he caused quite a commotion for a while. It seemed like every day he was running away, although he wouldn't go very far. A few blocks or so or maybe up in an old oak tree, just whatever worked for him at the time. His new parents were very good to him as they gave him space and didn't make a big deal out of him running away since they knew he'd be back for supper. Guess he felt it was a game he was supposed to play called the kid nobody wanted until now and he had to be sure it was for real. And he was good at playing it.

I met him on one of those running away from home trips when he hid in an old shed behind my house. Guess I scared him as much as he did me when I walked in to play cowboys with my chrome pistol. When he saw the pistol he started screaming. Hell, it scared me too. He finally just curled up and was crying. I guess even then I knew there was more to it than I realized. I put my pistol back in my holster and went over to him.

"What's wrong with you? Why are you crying?"

He looked up at me, "I don't want you to shoot my parents! I don't want to go away again!"

"I don't know what you mean. Look, it's only a play gun."

I held it my hand on it, “It's not a real gun, see.”

I pulled it out and squeezed the trigger only making a snapping noise. He calmed down some and we started talking. He pulled out his billfold he carried in his front pants pocket. He said he learned in the home he was in you carried the things you wanted most in your front pockets since things in your back pockets would get stolen or go missing. He told me it was the only thing he had left from his old home. It was just an old black and white photograph with him sitting in a chair with a baby in his lap. He proudly pointed at the baby in the photo.

“That's my brother, Bobby. I don't remember much about him, only his name.”

“Why don't you know much about him? Doesn't he live with you and your mom and dad like my little sister lives with us?”

“My mom and dad are gone. Someone came and shot them one night with a pistol like you have. That's when the people came and got me and my brother. They took us to a new place to live.”

I remember asking, “Was your dad a cowboy? You know all the stuff you see on TV is not real. The Lone Ranger never really hurts anyone and I bet your mom and dad was just playing like on TV. They'll probably come get you soon, I just bet on it.”

He looked at me with a sparkle in his eyes, “I hope so, but it's been a long time and I haven't seen them or my brother since then.”

I wish they would come back because I'm tired of playing this game. I miss them so much. I’m beginning to have a hard time remembering their faces and already can’t remember my parent’s names, only momma and daddy. My new parents can’t tell me what their names are either. I feel like my life until now is not real, only a dream.

“So that would be the beginning of my lifelong friendship with Hammer. Mike, to answer your question about did I know him?” Gravedigger paused for a moment in thought.

"Maybe I did about as well as anyone. Although he probably didn't know his own life as well as he would have liked."

He always had questions he knew would never have answers. But he never gave up on finding his brother. You see he was the first one of us to decide to drive a truck. Not because he wanted to, but rather he felt it would give him the best opportunity someday to run up on his brother. You have to admit one fact, Rookie. When you consider it you do meet and see a lot more people driving a truck than just about any other job. His hopes were one day he'd meet someone would turn out to be Bobby. Anything, because hope was surely the one thing he had in abundance.

John spoke up wiping his eyes, "I knew about Hammer having a brother and always looking for some link to find him. I never knew about his parents being killed this way, only he was adopted. Guess I learned something new also, Rookie. Thanks for sharing your story with us, Gravedigger."

"Guess there was never a reason to talk about it before, Big John. To be honest I don't know what made me think about it now. I do know I miss my friend Hammer and would love to see him again. Maybe if I'm good enough I will someday. No need to thank me, Big John. You have to understand I enjoyed the walk down memory lane as well."

They all chuckled a little and it was time to move on in and load. After getting loaded John, Mike and Bill shook hands and were off on another run. Such is the life of a truck driver.

The old truck stop at Bee Bayou was not much to look at. But it had good food and something else you couldn't find anywhere else on earth. It was known to have the most interesting waitress in the world, Ursula. She was born and raised in Germany where her family ran a small store and restaurant. She met and married an American soldier, moved to the States and settled down with him in Louisiana. She could speak very little English when she first arrived and soon was pregnant with their first child. One day her husband came home from work and told her the local ladies were going to come over Saturday to give her a baby shower. Well, since there were no such events in Germany and with her husband not being able to speak sufficient German plus with her little understanding of English or American customs somewhere in the translation she finally got across to her husband she was more than capable of bathing herself! And if those ladies came over to her house she would kick their tales for them! Yes, Ursula was a diamond in the rough who became probably one of the best known and most loved waitresses in the trucking world. She would keep you laughing from the time you arrived until the time you left. She once told a driver she was bisexual.

"Ursula, don't believe I would be telling that!"

"No, I'm serious. Every time I mention sex to a man he always says BYE!"

John could not miss this opportunity to see the reaction on Mikes face when meeting Ursula for the first time. They walked in and sat down. John quickly picked up a menu, partly to read, but mostly to hide his face so Mike could not see him smile or snicker. Ursula walked over to the table and in her usual comedic manner greeted them.

"Oh, it's you again so what did you bring me?" she asked John.

She quickly looked at Mike, "Oh, fresh meat," while rubbing her hands together and smacking her lips.

Mike was completely astonished. He looked up from his menu at Ursula who had a devilish grin on her face and at John who was doing all he could not to burst out laughing.

Mike blew it off, "Believe I'll start with coffee for now."

"Think I will too," replied John.

She came back with their coffee and asked for their order.

Mike nervously ordered first, “Think I'll have the hamburger steak with mashed potatoes.”

“Believe I'll have the same, Ursula.”

While they were waiting on their orders Ursula came back with the coffee pot to fill the cups.

She stood there a while then asked Mike, “Have you ever had a knock down, drop dead gorgeous hot waitress sit on you and kiss your cheeks?” John started to laugh.

Mike, completely shocked just sat there with his mouth wide open. “No, honestly can’t say I have.”

Ursula sat down and slid over toward him as he tried to slide away and then she leaned over, pecked his cheek and got up laughing.

“Well, I suppose I have now, huh?”

Ursula giggled with her usual devilish grin, “No honey, you still haven't, but I appreciate the compliment!”

Mike's face was as red as a fire engine since he had no idea how to handle this situation.

John could see his embarrassment, “Everyone out here has a first time experience with Ursula and always have to come back to see her again. She's the last of a dying breed.”

After having his first experience with Ursula, Mike was still scratching his head with wonder. He had never met anyone like her in his life. You just couldn't help but like her. She was like your favorite grandmother, aunt, neighbor and family friend all rolled into one neat package. John sat and told stories he knew about her as Mike drove across Louisiana.

Mike noted on how rough the roads were in Louisiana. John said they have been rough for as long as he could remember. Somehow it seems the road use tax money from the Federal Government never makes it to the highways! It's always been this way. After they got into Texas Mike noticed the highways were much better and smoother. John said Texas took a little bit more care of their roads than most did. It all depended on the state and how much Federal money actually made it to the roads.

It was after midnight as they went through Longview. A few more miles up the road Mike was driving along when all of a sudden he locked up the brakes and cried, “What the blazes?”

John jumped up and saw a skinny young woman run out in front of the truck as they went by the picnic area. “Sorry Rookie, I should have warned you, but I forgot.”

There are some hookers who work these two picnic areas here. They will run across the interstate from one side to the other all night. There have been quite a few to get struck and killed here before. But it seems there's always another one to take their place.

Mike grabbed another gear and started going again. “I'm sure glad I didn't hit her. Don't think I could have lived with it, even if she was a hooker.”

“You have to be on your toes out here kid. You just never know what may happen at any given moment.”

Mike took a moment and tried to shake it off. He was learning whenever an emergency situation happened it causes adrenaline to release into your system. Afterward the effects can be hard to deal with. Your heart will race, your arms and legs suddenly weaken and seems you can't catch your breath and sometimes your vision will blur. A little while later is the headaches you think will last forever. It all depends on the severity of the emergency as to the extent of the effects.

Still trying to shake it off he asked John, “What do you think makes a woman want to do something such as that? You know, become a prostitute.”

John shook his head slowly, lit a cigarette and sighed, “That is a question often asked since the dawn of time I suppose.”

I've been around them so long now I hardly give it a second thought. That's probably why I didn't mention the picnic area earlier. I guess since you have a daughter it probably plays more on your mind than it would mine. After all, the fact is they are all someone's daughter.

"That's true, John. It does play on my mind."

I love all my children and have tried hard to instill God into their lives as my parents did for me. How can a child of God turn to such a Godless act as this? As you said they are someone's daughter as well. I can't say with all certainty my daughter would never do this, I only pray to God she lives a Christian life should something happen to Susan or me.

"Mike, I wish I had the answer for you would inoculate your daughter like a vaccine against this happening."

The fact is things happen in their lives to cause these women to choose this life style. In all cases it was not a wanted decision on their part. Sex for them is not a pleasure, but rather a means of survival. Most of these girls you will see out here are addicted to some type of drug costing far more than most jobs pay. If the truth be known, most of these women did not come from poor homes. They didn't come from broken homes. They weren't abused as children by fathers, uncles or neighbors. I'm sure some of those situations could be contributing factors in a few cases, but these type of situations cause most women to be more aware and more cautious of men along with less likely to meet with or have relations with a stranger. Money is the root of the action. Drugs are most often the cause.

"How do you know so much about this, John?"

John took a long hard look at Mike, "Let's say it's a personal matter I don't care to discuss with you. Perhaps one day if the time is right and I feel you need and deserve an answer I'll share some of the pain in my life with you. For now just hold and love your daughter."

In the dark Mike couldn't tell much about the lay of the land in this part of Texas, but he already knew it was hillier than the Houston area. They stopped at the Knox truck stop in Mesquite to rest a while until the business opened for their delivery. John had never been there before and needed to get directions to them. Mike thought the place was just a little dirty, but it would do for now. They went inside and ate breakfast. John said they didn't know when they would get a chance to eat again plus it could be a very long day.

It took a while for them to get unloaded, but once they were they called dispatch. They were sent to Midlothian to load at the steel mill for Piney Flatt, Tennessee. As they pulled onto the road leading to the mill instead of turning right into the main gate entrance John turned left into a parking lot across from it.

Mike was baffled and asked John, “Why are we stopping here and not going into the plant?”

“This will be your first dealing with a freight broker. We have to go here first to get our gate pass and information for our load. There are very few carriers who pull directly out of the mill here. Most have to go through this or another broker to get their loads.”

Mike was still a little confused, “I don't get it. Why would the mill do this instead of dealing directly with the carriers?”

John took on a more serious look and explained. You see the mill doesn't want to deal with keeping up with all the carriers it will need to move the freight to their customers. So they turn it over to one or in some cases a hand full of brokers to hand it out to who they want at the rate they want to pay. Just like with a lot of businesses we deal with it goes through several hands before we get it. Each one is palm up, meaning they take a lion’s share of the revenue leaving us the leftovers.

“That doesn't seem right.”

“That's just the way it is and I don't see it changing anytime soon kid. These people aren't bad. Hell I even considered leasing to them when I had my truck one time. But I couldn't find enough freight where their loads went to get me back here so it wouldn't work out. They're still good people here."

After getting loaded and chaining down the round bars Mike and John hit the road again. They pulled off in Terrell at Rip Griffins truck stop to eat a late dinner. Mike looked around at the huge parking lot and the size of the main building. They walked inside to eat dinner.

"This place is almost as big as the one on the west side of Wyoming, The Little America."

"Yeah, but I believe you'll find we come a lot closer to being able to afford to eat here than there!"

Mike looked at the menu, "I see what you mean, Big John."

They ordered their meals and where sitting, looking around the room. John all of a sudden got an unmistakable far away and sad look in his eye.

Mike watched him for a moment, "What's the matter, John? You look like you just lost your best friend."

John looked at Mike, "Yeah, you're right. It just hit me we're going to Piney Flatt, Tennessee. That's just a few miles from where I did lose my best friend, Hammer Lane!"

"John, I noticed a Chapel outside as we walked in. Perhaps a few moments in God's house will give you the strength you need. He can always help with times such as this."

"Now Rookie!" just then John stopped before finishing his comment. He looked around the room at the other drivers and tourists enjoying their meals. "I really like you kid."

I appreciate the fact you have so much faith in your God. But this is an area I don't care to discuss with you or anyone else for that matter. I'm not saying you're wrong or I'm right. I will say this, if there should come a time when I need someone to preach to me you may be the first one I talk to. For now concern yourself with your own soul and leave mine the Hell out of it. Let's get out of here and go to Birmingham so you can go home.

Chapter Four

Hidden Dangers

The trip across Texas, Louisiana and Mississippi went well. Traffic was light and the Smokey Bears where few. Mike was settling in to his new career as a truck driver and beginning to feel a little more confident. He thought back on the last month or so and contemplated as to whether he made the right decisions under pressure. He thought, I haven't hurt or killed anyone yet, so far so good. Finally the Alabama State Line and Sweet Home was in site as he felt it was about time. A hundred and twenty one miles and he'd be at the home terminal and go home for a little while since the load didn't have to be in Tennessee until Monday. John was asleep in the back and the radio was quiet so he could get lost in his thoughts at the moment.

As Mike pulled into a parking spot at the terminal he thought how quickly the trip went. He got out and went over to the guard house to talk with the guard a little while.

"Trying to work your dope down, huh?" inquired the guard.

"What are you talking about?"

"Are you for real, you really don't know?"

"I don't know what you mean?"

The guard stood back a little, "You've never heard the old expression trying to kill my dope before, for real?"

"No, I really don't know what you are talking about."

The guard explained to Mike it was a terminology used when you have taken some stay alert pills or road dope and are waiting for it to wear off so you can go to sleep. Mike said he didn't take anything to stay awake and never would because it was illegal.

"In case you change your mind one day come see me. That's part of why I'm here."

Mike looked at him bewildered, "If you say so. Guess I need to go lay my head over the wheel a while. My partner's asleep in the bed."

"Oh, you're a trainee. I didn't know. Forget what I said for now. Except the part about if you need help then come look me up." Mike acknowledged him and went back to the truck.

As John and Mike walked into the dispatch a red headed lady called out to John to come into her office a minute. "And bring the kid with you."

"Morning Ms. Mary," said John. "How are you today?"

"Too early to tell, I haven't had my third cup of coffee."

Mike sat in the corner and looked around the room. There were a few things with the company logo on them otherwise the office was kind of plain looking to him. There were no pictures of children or people of any sort for that matter. It was almost a sad thing he thought.

"How's the kid doing, is he ready yet?"

"Well he ain't bad, but he ain't real good either."

She looked at Mike, "How do you feel kid, think you're ready?"

"That's up to John."

"I didn't ask John, I asked you."

"Yes ma'am."

"Besides it's up to me. Not you or him."

"Yes ma'am."

"Since I'm the owner don't you think?"

"Yes ma'am."

"My name is Mary. Not ma'am. Remember that!"

"Yes ma'am, I mean Mary!"

They all laughed as John asked, "You need him now?"

She took a long breath, "I have another one from the school he went to wants to hire in. I just thought it would be a good time to swap out while you were here this weekend."

"I guess so. He could learn a little more, but then again he can learn on his own."

"Good then it's settled. Mike, you'll come in here first thing Monday morning and I'll have you a truck. Just don't let me down, honey. We've invested quite a lot of time and money in you already."

"Yes ma'am," answered Mike, "I won't dare let you down, be here first thing."

Mary shook her head and beamed angry eyes toward Mike who quickly added, "Ms. Mary!"

As they walked out to the parking lot Mike told John how much he appreciated his time and patience with him.

"If you think I'm going to hug you and give you a kiss you better think again!" They both chuckled as Mike went to get in his pickup to leave.

He told John, "I guess I'll see you Monday, John."

"No you won't kid. I've got to be in Piney Flatt with my new trainee, remember."

Mike thought that's right as it suddenly hit him he would be completely on his own come Monday. It was a very sobering feeling and one he surely would experience quite often in this new career. He sat quietly in his little pickup reflecting on the past few weeks. Everything was so fast paced in this trucking life of which he found himself a part. All he experienced lately gave him much to ponder this weekend.

"Daddy's home!" cried the boys as they stepped down from the school bus. Josh, the oldest went to check the mail box sitting by the road at the end of their driveway. It was something he assigned himself to do ever since he was a little boy when they first moved there. Willy, his younger brother was running to the house to see his dad. Willy was a free spirited boy who had his own way of doing things. Mike sometimes felt Willy would do exactly opposite you thought he would just to be different. Willy was very active, but also very small for his age.

Mike was constantly telling him, "Slow down Peanut, you're not giving yourself time to grow!"

Yes, everyone called Willy "Peanut" because of his small stature. And as usual Peanut was the first one in the door and on his dad's lap beside his sister, Crystal. She was the light of her dad's eyes. She was considered their miracle child. After having Willy the doctor told Mike and his wife Susan she would never have children again and recommended she have a hysterectomy to avoid problems later. They both decided if it was God's plan then so be it. But for now they would give Him time to make the decision. A few years later they got their answer, Crystal! Josh came up walking in his usual manly manner as Mike had a hard time trying to remember when Josh didn't have such an air of confidence about him.

Josh walked over to his dad and handed him the mail. "Don't think there's anything but junk mail, Daddy. How did your week go, see anything interesting?"

Mike looked at Josh a moment thinking he sure is growing into a fine young man. "Yeah I had a good week and I have a surprise, too?"

"What's that Daddy?" they all asked.

"I get my own truck to drive Monday." Mike smiled at them.

"Then I guess you can tell your friends your dad will officially be a truck driver when you go back to school."

Crystal reached up and grabbed her dad's cheek. "Can you take me for a ride in it, Daddy?"

Mike smiled at her, "Sure honey, but you'll have to wait until I get home with it."

Then the phone rang and Peanut ran to answered it. "Hello," he said. Then he got a surprised look on his face, "Yes sir and please hold on a minute, I'll get him. Daddy, it's for you."

Mike walked over to the phone, "Hello."

Then he heard John's voice on the other end. "I see you made it home so you must have remembered how to get there."

"Yeah, what's going on John?"

John paused a second, "Afraid there's been a change in plans, Mike."

One of our trucks broke down in Memphis and we have to send the truck Mary was going to assign you up there and bring the other back. So there won't be a truck for you until we get that one fixed. Mary wanted me to call and tell you, also to see what you wanted to do. We don't know how long it will take to get the other truck fixed since we think the motor's bad. You can stay home until it's fixed or you can go out with me until then if you need to work. The upside is you won't be on training pay of two hundred and fifty dollars a week as before, but rather you'll be paid the second driver rate of twelve cents per mile on all miles you and I both drive. Believe me it will be more than what you were making before.

Mike thought a moment, "I suppose this is something can't be helped so what do I need to do, Big John?"

"That's up to you kid since you're the only one knows your financial situation. Do you need to work or not?"

"Of course I do, John. What I meant is what you need me to do, come back up there or get with you Sunday sometime?"

"No you stay home and enjoy your family time. I'll stay here in town for the weekend and we'll leave around dark Sunday."

"Sure, see you then."

Mike hung up the phone then turned around to his kids "Seems I'm going to have to wait a little longer to get my own truck," as he explained the situation to them. "You can still say your dad is an official truck driver now since I will be second driver on a team."

The kids started to dance around saying, "Yea, Daddy's a trucker now!"

Mike looked at all his children and thought to himself, God truly has blessed me beyond belief.

Sunday came faster than ever before thought Mike. He didn't know why being a driver made a difference, but it did. He just couldn't seem to get enough home time and it was getting harder and harder to leave when it was time to go. And it didn't seem to affect only him. His wife and the kids were all getting restless as the time to go was drawing near. They had always enjoyed going to their small local Church every Sunday and still do, but it now signaled it would soon be time for Daddy to leave out on a trip again. Mike didn't consider himself to be an extremely religious man, but he did keep God in his daily life relying on his wisdom for support in all his decisions. He thought how strange the one day of the week set aside for the Lord is the one day of the week man would decide Mike, as a truck driver, would have to leave his family and work. But feeling as blessed by God as he was could only believe He was in agreement with Mike's new job or He wouldn't have allowed it to come to pass. As they were sitting around talking and getting ready for Mike to leave the phone rang.

As usual Peanut beat everyone else to the phone. "Hello," then Peanut suddenly got an excited tone in his voice.

"Uncle Bob, where have you been?"

There was a pause and then Peanut said, "I missed you, why haven't you been by to see me? We've all been looking for you. Okay, I'll get Daddy for you."

Mike picked up the phone, "Hello stranger, been awhile."

"I've been busy lately and took some time off with a friend in Montana for a few weeks."

"Montana! I was in Montana a few weeks ago. Wish I had known may have run into you there."

"It happens sometimes. You never know who you may run into or what."

"Yeah, thought I saw you in Whiteland, Indiana at the Stop 99 truck stop a few weeks ago."

"Don't remember being there in quite a while, wasn't me."

"I could have sworn it was you, guess I was mistaken."

"How is the training going, are they about ready to give you a truck?"

"It's going good. In fact I was supposed to get my own truck Monday, but they had a truck break down in Memphis and had to send the one I was to get up there. So now I have to ride with Big John a little longer. But they did take me off training pay and made me second driver."

"That's good, be a little more money for you. How are you dealing with the driving? Are you starting to get used to leaving home?"

"Funny you should ask as we were just talking about this when you called. We can't seem to get adjusted. Does it ever get any better, Bob?"

"As long as you have a family and a home you will always have a hard time leaving them. Do you know what is worse, Mike?"

"I really can't imagine anything worse."

Bob hesitated a second then quickly added.

"Not having a family or home to miss!"

"As usual Bob, you helped me put things in perspective and gave me a way to cope with my problems. Are you sure you're not one of God's angels sent down to help me and my family?"

"If you only knew you'd never say that, Mike. I'm anything but!"

"How was your weekend?" John asked as Mike grabbed his bag and clothes from the pickup.

"It went well and as usual fast!" Mike then went and parked his pickup and walked back to the truck.

"Hate things didn't work out so you'd get your own truck, but that's life out here. Always changing so you have to adjust and drive on."

"I was looking forward to it, but everything happens for a reason and I just have to accept it. By the way Bob called just before I left. He said it was not him in Indiana that day."

"Where was he at when you talked with him?"

"That's funny, he didn't say and I didn't ask. Wonder how that could happen?"

"Can't say, but guess it does now and then. We just get caught up in the moment I suppose and forget to ask. We better get out of here since time's a wasting."

They climbed in the cab and Mike put it in gear then pulled out of the yard. It was a beginning of another week on the road and they both couldn't help but wonder where it would lead them.

"I've heard of them before, but I've not been there," John mentioned while he was on the phone with dispatch after unloading in Piney Flatt. He wrote the information down and hung up the phone. John always hated going to a new shipper.

He then turned around to Mike, "We've got to head for Florida Steel in Knoxville and pick up a load to Benton, Arkansas. We're going to have to get close to town and call for directions since I haven't been there before."

They drove back down toward Knoxville and stopped at a fuel stop just outside of town where they called for directions to the plant. It was around noon when they finally got to the mill and checked in.

John looked around, "Different steel mill, different town, but the same old bull crap, sit and wait!"

Mike was beginning to understand exactly what he meant as he looked around at all the trucks waiting to get loaded. "You never told me the story of how Hammer and Mary got together. Think if you want there should be time now from the look of things here."

John sat back in the seat a little, "After the incident with the rapist in Greenwood, Mary had a problem getting going again."

I suppose it was understandable given what happened there. Her sister in Longview was a big help for her giving her support and understanding. But considering the strong woman she is it wasn't long until Mary started to get it turned around and decided to go back to work. As I said before she lost the dedicated run from Birmingham to Dallas and back. By the time she was ready to go back to work there was already someone else on it. So she started to go where she could much as we do and one day took a load from La Place, Louisiana to Greenville, North Carolina. While she was there at the steel mill in La Place getting loaded she happened to notice a black Kenworth W 900 conventional sitting loaded outside the gate. She couldn't remember who drove it, but it looked very familiar to her. She assumed since it hadn't moved for a long time and she'd not seen anyone around it the driver must be taking a nap in the sleeper. Perhaps she may see who it was before she left. She went into the steel mill to load.

It took quite a while to get loaded as usual, but she finally was done and could go outside the gate to tarp down. She pulled across the scales and got her paper work then pulled outside the gate and parked alongside the roadway. She pulled out her chains and secured the load. Then she climbed up on the steel and started rolling out her tarps. Everything was going well until she was standing on the edge of the trailer trying to spread the tarp over the edge. All of a sudden she lost her footing and fell backwards off the trailer. There was nothing she could do but accept the fact she was about to land flat on her back on the ground and probably break something. Or at the least bruise something bad and be in pain for some time. Just before she hit the ground she felt someone's arms wrap around her and pull her to their chest as they hit the ground with her on top. After it was over she got up and turned around.

"Well I be damned it's you, pig face!"

Yes, it was Hammer who had just gotten up from his nap and was going to the restroom. He looked at her a moment then walked off toward the restroom. Mary stood there and couldn't believe he would just leave and not comment on the matter. As Hammer walked back toward his truck he stopped at Mary's to watch her finish covering her load.

For a moment Mary stopped what she was doing, "You ain't talking much today. Why did you just walk off a while ago and not say a word?"

"Had to pee and I knew you wouldn't be going anywhere."

"Well guess that's twice you helped me out. Suppose you think I owe you something now, huh?"

"Only if you think you do."

Mary giggled, "I suppose I could at least buy your dinner for you."

"Don't believe I've ever had a woman buy me a meal before. Don't think I know how to take that."

"All I can do is offer. You don't have to accept it!"

Mary was getting a little angry now.

Hammer blew it off, "Where are you going?"

"Greenville, North Carolina. And you?"

"Winston Salem."

Mary went to get in her truck and turned around looking back at Hammer, "Now how about this, first one to get to the Supper Club in McNeal, Mississippi buys dinner?"

With that they were off. Afterwards they were inseparable. Even though they came from different worlds they had a bond between them could stand the test of time. They were married a year later and started the company. The rest is history.

The sun was going down as John and Mike finished securing the load. It had been a very long day and they were ready for a meal since they were unable to eat earlier. They stopped at the TA truck stop, got parked and went inside.

Mike noticed the Cowboy Boot Outlet Store across the street from the truck stop. "Is that store for real, or a rip off?"

"No, it's for real, just a little pricey for me"

"What do you consider pricey, John?"

"Oh, anything over fifty bucks. They have some over seven hundred. So what do you think kid?"

"Wow! Now that is just a little too much for this poor Alabama boy!"

They went in and ordered dinner. After their meal they sat back a minute and reflected on the day.

"How long will it take to get to Benton, John?"

John took a sip of his coffee, "Around eight and a half hours, give or take."

"I had a little talk with the security guard the other night at the yard."

"You mean Jason?" asked John curiously.

"The one works at night, I actually didn't get his name."

"Yeah, that's Jason. Been with us a long time, almost from the start," explained John. "He used to be a driver long ago. He had a bad wreck and lost his sight in one eye. That disqualified him to drive anymore so Hammer kept him on as a guard."

"He was talking to me about road dope and I didn't exactly know what to say."

"Road dope, are you sure about that kid? He was asking you for road dope?"

"No, he implied if I needed it, he would be able to get it."

"Well I never!"

Mike sat there thinking and getting the feeling he was the butt of a joke somehow and not quite able to figure out what it was.

"Am I missing something here, Big John?"

John sipped some more coffee, "I suppose it's time you learn about your pocket co-driver."

It's a personal decision one day you'll need to make on your own. If you intend to run hard and make more money you are going to come up on the problem of too many miles and not enough time to sleep. Now this could be one of those situations here if you were on your own. It's late and you've been up all day waiting to get loaded and the customer wants his load in Benton at first light. It's about eight and a half hours to where you are going and it is now 9:30 pm out there. Meaning if you left right now you would be there around 6:00 am. The way you feel right at this moment can you drive all night and stay awake? And by staying awake I also mean ALERT!

"I think I can, but how can I be sure at this moment what I'll feel later?"

"You can't so when you start to get sleepy or realize you're not as alert as you should be you will wake me up and have me drive."

What are you going to do when there's no one else in the truck and you have the same problem? There are two choices.

Stop and go to sleep hoping after a hard day you can wake up in time to get to Benton tomorrow evening to get unloaded. Bear in mind even if you do the chances of getting another load are all but gone. This means you will have to lay over there and wait until the next day to load losing a day's pay. Or you take a little something to stay awake and most of all ALERT and go on to Benton. Unload and find another load. Get loaded then hopefully take a nap somewhere. Don't get me wrong kid if you just can't go on you go to bed. Everyone has their breaking point and only you know when it is. As I said before you can do everything out here by the book and strictly legal and go from job to job to job because either you can't get the load there when it has to be or you can't make enough money to support your family. It really shouldn't be this way, Mike. But this is the real world as it is now and until something happens to change the way shipper's ship, receivers receive and governments govern this is how it will be. The choice is yours and only you can make it.

I will say you're lucky you work for one of the few companies the powers that be, meaning Ms. Mary, who know what it's like out here and will back you up as long as you're honest with them. And will understand if you simply can't get the job done when there's a problem. But that's only part of the job. You still have to deal with the shippers who couldn't care less how you feel or how long you have to wait on them. Or how hard you have to work to secure their freight or anything else involved. Then you have the receiver who has the same attitude when it comes to you as the shipper does. If you're late it's your fault and this is all that matters to them. No other explanation accepted.

Mike shook his head as he looked hard at John, "This is going to take a long time to think over. It goes against everything I believe in and stand for as a father, a husband and a Christian, John."

"I understand. To be honest with you I don't like it either."

But as I said before it's a personal decision. The same as the decision you made whether to continue to work in a tire shop for less than it takes to raise your family or learn to drive a truck for a decent living. The choice is yours to make. "Now let's get out of here and get to Arkansas," as John finished his coffee.

After getting in the truck Mike adjusted the seat and mirror. He turned on the CB just in time to hear someone say, "Break one-nine! Any of you drivers looking for go fast, nose candy or some smoking dope take it to Harley."

"What the blazes? What is this all about, John?"

"Those are lowlifes trying to sell cocaine, methamphetamine and marijuana on the CB."

Harley, is channel one. You know as in the Harley Davidson logo, Harley 1. It's all an idiotic code trying to keep the cops from finding them as if the cops are this dumb. More importantly it brings me to another matter. The drugs those idiots' are trying to sell ARE NOT what we discussed earlier. What I was referring to are prescription or over the counter pills to my knowledge are not addictive. At least I never felt I had to have them to function every day. The drugs they're trying to sell Rookie, that's a totally different matter. Not to throw off on you kid, but what they're trying to push was never a problem until this new breed of driver from the truck driving schools which kept popping up everywhere and began spitting them out left and right. To put it to you as plain as I can if I ever catch you fooling with the crap those idiots' push, I will put a whooping on you your daddy will be proud of. Do we understand each other?

"Fair enough, let's go," as Mike let out on the clutch.

Just as John thought would happen Mike woke him up east of Nashville in a rest area he stopped at and asked if John would be able to drive now.

"I guess you know more about what I was telling you earlier."

Mike just nodded his head, "Don't care right now. I just want to sleep for a while."

John took over and it wasn't long before he could hear Mike snoring in the sleeper. John enjoyed driving along Interstate 40 talking to the other truckers on the CB while they were moving America from one place to another one piece at a time. Interstate 40 is considered a main hub of commerce in America stretching all the way from Raleigh, North Carolina to Barstow, California. In fact some people consider Memphis, Tennessee to be "Hub City" for that reason. It is where Interstate 40 stretching from almost the east coast to almost the west coast and Interstate 55 stretching from almost the Gulf of Mexico to the Great Lakes intersect. And don't forget about "The Blues Highway", US Highway 61 called so because of the delta towns it runs through on the way to Chicago. It was the route so many of the farm workers took to go north for a better life and also the heart and soul of blues music. And US Highway 78, stretching across the southern states east to west commonly called the "Tallulah Bankhead Highway", after the great lady of the south.

Yes, this area was rich in history from long ago and even to the present. Such was the birth of Rock and Roll. Elvis Presley, Carl Perkins, Johnny Cash, Roy Orbison, Jerry Lee Lewis and the list goes on and on. Memphis was a very special place he was going through right now. As he went over the Mississippi River he looked out into the night at the lights, the sparkle and reflection of the lights on "Old Man River" as it has been called. The stuff a young man's dreams are made of. One interesting person enjoyed many adventures on the river in Hannibal, Missouri. Samuel Clemens loved his homeland and is known best by his pen name, "Mark Twain". Halfway across was a sign stating "Welcome to Arkansas, William "Bill" Clinton, Governor" and John knew to slow down and to keep his eyes open. This was one state which had very little use for trucks other than revenue enhancement. As usual the weigh station was backed up and it took a little while to get through, but once he was things would be back to normal. A little over an hour and a half and he would be in Benton.

"You sleep well?" asked John as Mike climbed out of the sleeper and stretched.

"Okay I guess, although the roads are a little rough here in Arkansas."

"I guess that's the one thing Louisiana is thankful for, Arkansas!"

It keeps Louisiana from having the reputation as the worst kept interstate system in the nation. Arkansas does have so many different taxes concerning trucks it's hard to keep up with them. I know it's one of, if not the most expensive states in the Union to operate a truck in. For the money they take in from the trucking industry we should be riding on golden highways and not broken up concrete! Some say it's this new Governor they have. He has quite a reputation with the ladies. Guess he has to keep them up.

"How long have they been unloading us?" Mike asked.

"About ten minutes give or take. Shouldn't be much longer, they're working pretty fast so far."

"They got a rest room?"

"Sure, go up to the building there and walk inside, first door on the right."

After Mike came back John told him were to go to Little Rock and pick up for Atlanta. Soon they were on their way to the chain link fencing plant. The truck traffic was heavy at the plant and soon it was time to load.

"What kind of stuff is this?"

"It's fencing kid. It's for chain link fences. You can't tell?"

"Now you mention it I guess I can see it. They sure do load it funny. It looks kind of dangerous and tall, glad we don't have to tarp it."

"But we do kid!"

"No way, I thought you said this was chain link fencing! Every chain link fence I've seen was outside. Why would we have to tarp this crap?"

"Two reasons," explained John. "They don't want road film getting on it and most important they don't have to pay us to tarp it. This makes reason number one good enough for them."

"Now that sucks big time. Ain't it a little dangerous climbing up on this stuff and spreading out the tarps?"

John frowned, "Welcome to flatbed trailer trucking kid."

After they got the load strapped they got up on the load and John took the rear, Mike took the front and then started to roll out the two tarps it would take to cover the load. With the spurs and pole ends sticking up everywhere the tarps kept getting stuck when they would try to pull them over the load. Mike was on the front pulling backwards when all of a sudden the tarp gave way a little. Mike went flying off the load landing between the trailer and the tractor flat on his back on the catwalk frame section of the tractor.

John got down and went running to him, "Are you alright Mike?"

Mike just lay there and was trying to talk and couldn't catch his breath. His face was red and he couldn't move. He looked up at John gasping for air.

John climbed up by him and grabbed his shoulders, "Calm down and take easy breaths. You just got the wind knocked out of you. Relax and lay there while I go look for some help."

John ran over to the shipping office and told them he needed help. Mike, his partner, had fallen off the load.

"What would you like us to do?" asked an office worker.

"I don't know maybe come help me or call for some help you think!" replied John.

"Where are you at?" another worker asked.

John pointed out the window, "We're over by the fence in the green Peterbilt there. He's between the cab and the trailer on the frame."

They looked out the window, "You're going to have to move that truck. You're not supposed to tarp down on the yard. You've got to move it out on the street to finish covering it!"

"I came in here to get help for my partner and I am not worried about where the truck needs to be or where the load will be covered. In fact I couldn't care less about the load right now and I better be getting some help real soon or you may need to call the cops for some help yourself!"

"Are you threatening us, driver?"

"No, I'm promising you all Hell is going to break lose if I don't get some help real soon!"

About then a man came in and asked what's going on. John explained the situation to him and the man turned around to the people sitting at their desks.

"How about calling the fire department and get them to send the paramedics out here, NOW! That's all he wanted in the first place."

"Yes sir," they answered as one of them picked up the phone and called.

The man then turned around to John, "Now let's go see if we can help him until they get here."

They went back to where Mike was laying and started talking to him. The man asked, "Are you okay driver? Can you move at all?"

Mike was just beginning to get his breath back a little and tried to answer him. But all he could do was gasp.

The man then told him, "That's okay, driver. We've got help on the way. Is there anything you need right now?"

Mike shook his head, “No,” and then lay quietly. John was about as nervous as he had ever been in his life. This was a good kid and he didn't deserve to be in this situation. Soon the paramedics were there and started to working on Mike. They eased him out on a back board then into an ambulance that just arrived.

John turned to the man from the plant, “I really need to go with him, but I can't leave the truck like this.”

“Just lock it up and go. Here's my card, when you’re ready to leave call me. I'll come get you or make arrangements.”

“Are you sure it will be okay with the people here?”

“Sure it will. I'm the plant manager and everything is going to be alright, don't you worry.”

“You really had us worried kid,” as Mike lay on the hospital bed.

“I didn't mean to. I was just trying to do my job. How are we going to get back to the truck?”

“When you're ready we'll call a cab to take us back. You know you're going to have to wear that corset for a while until your ribs heal. I still don't think it's a good idea to have you riding in a truck across these rough ass roads in Arkansas.”

“I just don't want to stay in a hospital in a strange town for long, John.”

“Alright then if that's what you want. I'll go call for a cab.”

The plant manager met them at the gate and let them in. John and the manager finished putting the tarps on the load and soon they were ready to go.

John held out his hand to the manager who took it and said, “Sorry about your friend. I hope everything works out and he gets back to work soon.”

“I appreciate that and I appreciate all your help,” said John.

With that John climbed in and they were off.

After a while Mike called out to John, “Slow down on these rough roads. For God's sake I've got four fractured ribs back here!”

“Bet your wife won't put up with your whining!”

It took quite a while longer getting back to Birmingham than usual. John made frequent stops getting coffee to allow Mike time to relax without the constant jarring of the loaded truck. Although conventional trucks had a much better ride than a cab over truck it was still a heavy vehicle and seemed to find every pot hole and bump in the road. Mike would be so glad to get out of it when they got back to the terminal, it would be none too soon for him.

“Are you sure you don't want me to drive you home, you know I don't mind.”

“I'll be alright. I can take my time and stop along the way if I need to. Just go on and deliver the load in Atlanta, John. You don't want to have to stay there tonight.”

“Okay if you're sure about it I'll go on. But I'm going to have Mary call and check on you every day. You better be getting well and not working around the house!”

“Okay John, I'll be good. Now go before it's too late to get the load off,” Mike pleaded. And with that John left.

Mike went to his pickup and threw in his bags and slowly started to get in. He thought if anyone is watching they must think he looked like a ninety year old man trying to get in his truck! He laughed and then immediately stopped, laughing was one of the things making it hurt worse. The trip to Montgomery seemed longer than the trip from Little Rock. He never thought about it before, but his little pickup truck didn't ride very good at all. In fact it was a very hard ride and he would be glad to get out of it. He also thought when you're hurt or in pain you notice the little things more or at least more sensitive to them. It seemed every few miles he would have to stop and walk around a little to try and ease the pain.

It took him about three and a half hours to make the ninety minute drive, but finally he was home. It wouldn't be long and the kids would be home from school. Crystal would be mad at him since he didn't go by grandmas and get her. But there was no way he could see after her in his condition right now. Maybe she would understand. However Susan would be another matter. He wouldn't let them call and tell her about his accident since he was coming home anyway. He guessed they would all be surprised to see him when they got home. He took the pain pills the doctor in Little Rock gave him and decided to try and sleep some before everyone got home. He lay down across the bed then soon was out like a light.

"How are you, baby? Can I get you anything right now?" asked Susan.

Mike looked up and around the room. He was naked down to his underwear and under the sheets. He thought long and hard, but couldn't remember taking his clothes off or even getting in the bed. "How did I get in the bed?"

"Josh helped me take your clothes off and got you under the covers. You just sort of moaned and sighed the whole time. You don't remember any of it, do you?"

Mike grinned, "Not at all, how long have I been asleep?"

"I can't say since I don't know what time you got home, but it's about 10:30 right now."

Mike looked around, "Can't be that late, it's still daylight outside."

"It's 10:30 in the morning, Mike. You slept all night!"

"No way, I lay down probably around 2:00 in the evening."

Mike shook his head, "There's no way I slept that long!"

Susan laughed and just walked off. She stopped at the door and turned around, "If you need anything just call. I took the day off in case you couldn't take care of yourself. They told me you were in bad shape, but you would be alright."

Surprised, Mike asked, "They who?"

"Your boss lady, what's her name? Mary! She called the night it happened and told me. She also said you didn't want us told because you didn't want to worry us."

Mike just blurted out, "Darn," under his breath.

Susan smiled, "I guess you can forget about us knowing while Mary's in charge!"

John made it to Atlanta in time to deliver and loaded back in Fulton Industrial Park for Tulsa. On the way back he stopped at the yard in Birmingham for a shower. He called Mike and his son Willy answered.

"Hello."

"Is that you, Peanut?"

"Yes sir, do I know you?"

"This is Big John, your dad's partner. Is your dad were I can talk to him?"

"No sir, he's been asleep since I've been home and Momma won't let us wake him up."

"Well can I talk with your mom?"

"Sure, I'll go get her," Willy replied.

"Hello," answered Susan.

"Susan, this is John. How's Mike doing?"

"He's been asleep ever since I've been home. We haven't tried to wake him up, figured the longer he sleeps, the quicker he'll heal up."

"I just wanted to check on him. You can tell him I called. Is there anything I can do for you or the family?"

"No, I think we'll be alright. But thanks for asking John."

John was headed west through Memphis when he started to get tired. It had been a very long day for him and he had covered too many miles. He thought a minute and decided he would stop at the 76 truck stop in West Memphis and go to bed. He rode around the lot and found a spot about half way back to park. He went inside to the restaurant and sat at the bar beside another driver. Since John had taken stay alert pills earlier he ordered a grilled cheese sandwich with a glass of milk instead of coffee to counteract the medication. The milk coats the stomach and the cheese helps coat as well. The bread will soak up the residue of the pills. It was an old trucker trick from years ago. This would allow him to sleep.

The driver to his right had his back to him and was talking to another driver as John sat down. When John started telling the waitress what he wanted the man turned around to glance at John then turned back around to continue talking to the other driver. After a while the man turned back straight and John got a side look at him. The man obviously had been badly burned before and had some extremely bad scarring on his face. He wore dark wraparound sun glasses even though it was night and also a blue Detroit Tiger cap. He had no facial hair at all and talked in an almost whisper type tone which made it hard to understand him. Still there was something about his voice seemed vaguely familiar to John.

"Where're you headed driver?" asked John.

The man glanced at John then back forward.

"Oklahoma City."

"I'm headed for Tulsa, thought I'd take nap here for a while and show up the next morning."

"That right?" replied the driver. "I don't have to be there until tomorrow evening. Thought I'd drink some coffee and eat a sandwich and go on across Arkansas toward Oklahoma."

"Yeah, I thought about going on too," John replied as he tried to get a better look. "But been up all day and won't do much good to go in tomorrow evening, I'd still have to wait until the next day to load."

John looked closer at the man, "Don't I know you from somewhere?"

The man took a quick look at John, "I have that effect on people, got one of those familiar handsome faces. It's a curse looking as good as I do. But you don't look familiar so what's your handle, driver?"

"They call me Big John on the CB. And you?"

"They call me Freddie for some reason," as he sort of giggled.

John thought about how cruel some people can be and this man must have quite a lot of character to be able to joke like this about his condition. With that the man got up then pulled out some money and laid it under his check.

He then said to John, "Be careful and have a good night's sleep."

"Thanks driver, think every thing's going to be alright across there?"

"Well, kinda-sorta," said the driver.

Chills went up John's spine when he heard the man's comment. It was an expression he had not heard for years and was from an old friend from long ago. He thought a minute and looked to see where the man went. But too late, he was gone that quick. John finished his meal and went to the truck to try and sleep. He kept thinking about the expression the man used, kinda-sorta, over and over again. He heard it many times before, but as far as he could remember only from very few people until now. How strange could that be?

"You heard what the doctor said, stay off your feet and take it easy," Susan commanded with a no nonsense tone.

"I know, but it's so boring just to sit around and do nothing."

Mike wondered what John was up to since he didn't bother to tell Susan where he was going when he called and she didn't ask. Well, didn't matter any way as he was stuck at home with this tight wrap around his chest and it was getting old fast. It simply hurt and that is all there was to it. Crystal finally decided to take a nap and let daddy rest. He loved her dearly, but sometimes she could be a little much to take. His wife was quick to tell him, "You're the one who spoiled her now deal with it". And he knew she was right, but Crystal was definitely a daddy's girl which was alright with him. The boys would be home from school soon and Peanut will be fighting for a spot in daddy's lap, knowing this was something would have to be limited for now until he could heal up some. For now he was feeling weak and needed rest. He never knew cracked ribs could hurt so much and make you feel so bad.

The phone rang and Susan answered it, "Hello."

The lady on the other end said, "Susan, this is Mary. How is Mike doing today?"

"He's doing okay, Ms. Mary. We went to our doctor today and had him checked out. He told him to take it easy and stay off his feet for at least a week. We have to go back to the doctor next week and see if he's healing right."

"I'm going to send some paper work to you to fill out so we can get the workman's comp going for you. When you get it look it over and if there are any questions or problems call me personally and I will deal with it for you, okay?"

"You're too kind. You don't need to do this. Mary, we can handle it for now so don't worry about us."

"My people are my family, my only family and I look after them. Just indulge me and let me help when you need it."

"Yes ma'am, we do appreciate you. Just send the paper work and I'll handle it." Susan was shocked Mary was so helpful.

"Okay, tell Mike I called and we're all pulling for him, talk to you later."

Susan thought how nice this lady seemed to be and how lucky they were to have someone like her in charge. Susan enjoyed her job with the state, but wondered if the supervisors there would be as kind if, God forbid, something happened to her. Hopefully they would never find out.

"Honey, could I get you to bring me something cold to drink, please?" Mike asked.

"Sure thing, baby," said Susan as she went to the refrigerator.

While she was getting a soda for Mike, she heard a "thump" noise and ran into the bedroom.

There was Mike on the floor on hands and knees trying to get up.

"What's wrong, baby?"

"I don't know, I was getting up to go to the bathroom and got sort of light headed and fell down."

Susan went over and helped him up, "Do you think you hurt yourself again?"

"I don't think so. I landed on my side and caught myself best I could. Nothing seems to be hurting any more than it was."

"This doesn't seem right, cracked ribs shouldn't be doing this."

"Maybe I'm just weak or something."

Susan was puzzled by this and the one thing she knew was she would have to keep a close eye on him. Something was just not right here. She thought about it and realized Mike had been a little weak and sluggish for a while now way before this accident on the job. She wondered if there could be something else wrong.

As long as Susan had known Mike he was very energetic. Nothing ever slowed him down. Even after working all day at the tire store he always had enough energy to play with the children. Perhaps the stress of a complete career change was getting to him or maybe the added stress of the road and all the things he was experiencing had something to do with it. Whatever the reason Mike was going through noticeable changes now and it bothered and worried her.

The next day she took him back to the doctor for a closer look. The doctor said it could be simply the stress from the injury plus the trauma from the fall affecting his balance. For now what he needed most was rest and quiet. Susan agreed and took Mike home.

"You will do exactly as the doctor ordered, Mike."

"Yes ma'am, Ms. Susan!"

Susan popped the top of Mike's head then hugged him. He and the children were her world and anytime one was in need she was very concerned. Just part of being a mother she thought.

Hammer Lane Express

CHAPTER FIVE

TAKE THE GOOD WITH THE BAD

It was a long three weeks, but Mike seemed to be getting over his injury and hoped soon to return for work. Susan had taken Mike back to the doctor earlier, told of Mike's weak spells and how he had fallen. The doctor did some simple blood tests, found his white cell count elevated and put Mike on antibiotics to battle a possible infection. Today would tell the tale as they were going back to the doctor and see if he could go back on the job.

"Have you seen Crystal's teddy bear honey? Never mind, I found it, must have gotten kicked under the bed last night," as Mike gave the stuffed toy to his daughter. "Now keep up with him sweetheart, you don't need to lose him again."

Crystal walked out to the front room and sat down in her little chair in front of the TV. Susan was running around looking for her purse and car keys while Mike sipped on his second cup of coffee. Mike thought as he sipped on the coffee how before he started driving a truck he might drink one cup a day.

Susan was the coffee drinker in the family, but now it was him complaining when the pot was empty. He thought back a few weeks ago in Virginia when John told him get used to liking country music if he intended to drive a truck for very long. He gave it consideration for a moment then shook his head and thought it ain't happening!

Then Susan hastily directed, "Load up everyone. We're going to be late as it is."

"How do you feel today, Mike?" asked the doctor.

"I feel pretty good, ready to get back to work and get some rest. Susan keeps finding things for me to do you know."

Susan popped him on the shoulder, "Now that's not funny!"

The doctor smiled and asked Mike to remove his shirt. He examined Mike's chest area and asked if he felt any pain as he pressed on certain areas. Mike said he felt no bad pain, but in fact he actually did feel some pain.

"Do you still feel fatigued, weak or dizzy, Mike?" asked the doctor.

"No sir, I feel pretty much normal now. Just getting a little bored and tired of sitting at home during the day."

The doctor listened to Mike's heart and had him take a deep breath. He then ran the palm of his hand down the length of Mike's back from below his neck to the bottom of his spine. He asked Mike if he felt any pain or numbness as he did. Again, Mike said no.

The doctor pondered for a moment, "You appear to have healed well as far as the rib area, but I'm still concerned with the weak spell you had and the high white cell count as well. You say you feel okay now, Mike?"

"Yes sir, I feel fine now, just need to get back to work."

The doctor took a long look at Mike, "Okay, I want you to be careful and not take any unnecessary chances out there."

He then sternly looked at Mike, “Promise you will tell me about problems with feeling weak or fatigued.”

Mike nodded “yes”.

Susan added, “I will drag him kicking and screaming if I have to, doctor. I will definitely promise you this!”

“Dixie Carriers, how may I help you?” asked the operator at the terminal when Mike called.

“Yes, I need to speak to Ms. Mary, please.”

“May I ask who is calling?”

“Yes, tell her it's Mike Turner.”

Soon Mary picked up the phone, “Are you ready to go back to work kid?”

“Yes ma'am, soon as I can.”

Mary laughed, “You sure sound anxious to get back to work so what's wrong?”

Mike sounded confused, “There's nothing wrong ma'am, why would you think there is?”

“Oh, most people would milk the workman's comp for as long as they could and now you want to go back to work.”

“I'm afraid something will happen and you'll have to give my truck away.”

“When do you want to come back and get started?”

“Today's Thursday, do you think I should come in tomorrow or wait until Monday?”

“Enjoy your weekend with your family, I'll see you Monday.”

“Yes ma'am.”

“I’m not telling you again my name is not ma’am, it’s Mary!”

“Sorry Ms. Mary, I will see you early Monday morning.”

On Friday evening Mike was sitting in his favorite chair enjoying time with his family when the phone rang. Again there was a mad dash, but Peanut beat everyone to the phone as usual.

"Hello. Uncle Bob, where're you at?"

Susan went over to the phone and took it from Willy, "How's our second most favorite truck driver doing tonight?"

"I'm on my way to Montgomery to unload Monday and thought I'd come by tomorrow if you don't mind."

"If you try and stay away we'll hunt you down and hang you!"

Mike jumped up and went to the phone, "Honey, you're going to scare him off if you're not careful."

She handed Mike the phone, "Where are you? When will you be here?"

"I'm in Hammond, Louisiana right at the moment. I'll be in Montgomery early in the morning. You and the family feel like going fishing tomorrow?"

"Of course, why wouldn't we?"

"Then wake me up at the truck stop in the morning and we'll go to the lake."

"Good, look forward to it," as Mike ended the call.

Mike informed the family of Bob's plans and everyone got excited. The one thing they all enjoyed was fishing and riding in Uncle Bob's bass boat. Bob didn't have a home anywhere so he had Mike keep the boat he bought and on occasion they would all go to the lake for the day. The trips to the lake came second only to Christmas around the Turner household. Then as they were settling down to watch the TV the phone rang again.

Mike made the statement, "What did Bob forget this time?"

Willy answered the phone again then looked at his dad, "Its Big John, Daddy."

Mike went to the phone, "I wondered when I'd hear from you again. Where are you tonight?"

"I'm at the yard in Birmingham," replied John.

"I got here a little over an hour ago and thought I'd call to see how you were."

"Doing well, guess you know the doctor released me. I go back to work Monday. Where are you headed this weekend?"

"Yeah, Mary told me you were going back to work and to answer your question I'm empty and have to get work done on my truck. So I'll be here Monday when you get here."

"I suppose you have another trainee riding with you now. Are you getting along with him?"

"Actually I don't. The one I was supposed to train went to work somewhere else. There is another one supposed to start soon, but according to Mary he has some sort of personal problem to take care of."

"Well then where you staying and what are your plans for tomorrow?"

"I'll stay in the truck. No reason I can't run the engine to keep cool. Other than this I don't have any plans but kill time around here I guess."

"Why don't you come down here and go fishing with us. Bob's coming in and we're all going to the lake and taking his boat. It'll be a fun time for all."

"Guess I could borrow one of Mary's cars and come down. Do you think it'll be alright with Bob?"

"Why of course it will. You just don't know him, John. Bob's about as easy going as anyone you will ever meet."

"Okay then, what time do I need to be there?"

"About 9:00 am should do, don't you think?"

"Sounds good to me, see you then."

Mike sat back down in his chair and thought, tomorrow should be a very good day. My two close friends will finally get to meet.

It seemed the sun came up earlier than normal the next day. It appeared even God was anxious to get the fishing trip started.

It was hard to figure out who was the first to run into the bedroom and wake up mom and dad. Mike thought no man's life is complete until he opens his eyes to the smiles and laughter of his children crawling all over him in bed and a dog licking your face. Susan got out of bed and went into the kitchen to prepare breakfast for her family while Mike played with the kids and kept them occupied so they would stay out of their mother's way. After breakfast the kids were getting restless and bugging Mike to go and get Uncle Bob. Finally it was time to go to the truck stop. Mike loaded up the kids and left. Soon they were pulling into the old 76 truck stop and riding around the lot looking for Bob.

It was Willy who first cried out, "There's Uncle Bob's truck over there!"

Mike pulled up next to the Western Star and opened the car door to get out then looked back, "You kids stay in the car and I'll go wake up Uncle Bob."

It was something Bob asked him to do a long time ago when Mike first came to pick him up. He told Mike he didn't want the kids to see him without his sunglasses on. The kids accepted Bob as he was and never seemed bothered by his appearance. However, Bob was sure they would not understand the fact he didn't have eye brows or eye lashes. Bob felt the children might be upset and possibly have bad dreams from the shocking site. Mike told Bob not to under estimate his kids. They were all three very tough and would understand anything came up since they dearly loved their Uncle Bob. So this is what they decided to do just in case.

"Morning stranger," Mike greeted Bob climbing out of the sleeper.

Bob quickly grabbed his sunglasses and put them on, "Give me a second and I'll be ready. How are the kids this morning?"

"They're waiting on you as usual."

As Bob climbed into the car all the kids crowded next to him and were asking more questions than one man could answer. Mike just sat back and drove. He thoroughly enjoyed someone else being the center of their attention for a change. They parked and got out walking toward the house.

Susan met them at the door, “We've all missed you, why have you been away so long?”

Bob hugged her, “I've been a little busy and was also trying to give you and Mike time to get used to trucking life without distractions.”

Susan gave him one of those suspicious looks only a woman can do, “I suppose that's the story you're going to stick to, huh?”

“What do you think?”

Just then the phone rang and this time Josh beat Willy to it.

“Hello,” answered Josh. “Yes sir, I'll get him.” Josh informed his dad he had a phone call.

Mike picked up the phone, “Hello John, where are you?”

“I'm in Prattville at the fuel stop. How do I get there from here?”

Mike gave John directions to the house and hung the phone up. He went out to where Bob was busy gathering equipment, “I have a surprise for you.”

“Oh yeah and what would that be?”

“Got someone I want you to meet and he'll be here in a little while.”

Bewildered Bob asked, “And who would this be?”

“Think I'll wait till he gets here.”

It took a little while, but soon John came wheeling up the driveway after missing it and driving by once.

As he got out of the car Susan went to greet him. “Good to finally meet the one who's responsible for trying to make a truck driver out of my husband,” she exclaimed.

John felt a little embarrassed. “Now don't blame me, he'll be what he wants to be. I just tried to keep him out of trouble.”

"They're all around back, John. You can join them if you like. Mike, Bob and the kids are getting the boat ready. I'll have the lunch basket ready shortly and we can go. Did you have breakfast already? I have some sausage biscuits left over if you want one."

John smiled, "Please, sounds good. Got any coffee too?"

"Sure, come on in and I'll fix it for you."

Susan gave him a biscuit and cup of coffee. "You can take it out back to where they are if you want, I don't mind."

John walked outside to where Mike, Bob and the kids were. He walked up to them and Bob's back was to him when Mike announced, "There you are. What took so long, we're almost ready to go?"

John started to speak when Bob turned around and caught John's eye. They looked at each other a moment then Bob suddenly held out his hand, "I'm Bob Walker and you must be the one Mike was going to surprise me with."

John stood there a second and then took Bob's hand shake, "I'm Big John, least it's what everyone calls me, glad to meet you, Bob."

Mike excused himself, "I've got to go inside and get something. I will be right back. You two get acquainted while I'm gone."

When Mike left John looked at Bob and remarked, "It's a very small world, huh?"

"Guess it is. Did you make it to Tulsa like you wanted the other week?"

"Sure did. Did you make it to Oklahoma City the next evening?"

"Sure did."

They both stood there a while as each wondered where this would go from here.

Then Mike came back, "Susan's ready. Guess we all need to load up and go. Who wants to ride with whom?"

John quickly responded, “I suppose Bob and me can follow you in Mary's car if he wants.”

Bob glanced over at John, “Guess it will be alright with me then we can get to know each other a little on the way to the lake.”

Mike said, “What a beautiful day for a fishing trip. I’ve got my family and my two closest friends. What else could a man want?” John looked over at Bob.

“Yeah, I believe it's going to be a very interesting day.”

Bob replied, “You can say that again!”

“So what's up with you?” John asked Bob as they pulled onto the highway behind Mike and his family.

“Don't know what you mean, John,” answered Bob.

John frowned, “That night a few weeks ago in Whiteland at the Stop Ninety Nine. Mike saw you and you ran out. Now why would you do that?”

Bob looked at the scenery then replied, “Wasn't me, haven't been there in a long time just as I told Mike.”

“Bull crap!” exclaimed John. “I saw you before Mike pointed you out. It's not every day you see someone wearing sunglasses at night. At the time I just didn't know who you were. Now do you want to try again?”

Bob squirmed around in the seat then looked over at John and explained, “There are things at play here you don't know and also things you may not understand. But I do have my reasons, John. I just can't tell you what they are right now.”

John was getting a little mad at this point, “I really couldn't care less about what your reasons are, but I do care about Mike and his family. You aren’t running around with Susan behind Mike’s back are you? Because if you are I will hunt you down and send you to Hell myself!” Bob glanced over toward John.

"I can see where Mike thinks so much of you, John. And no, it has nothing to do with his beautiful wife."

There will come a time when all is revealed. It's just not here at the moment. There too many people involved who don't need the added stress at this time. I love this family more than you realize. They mean everything in the world to me. I could never hurt them intentionally, John. I hope you can appreciate that.

"Bob, I just don't understand all the secrecy."

It's like you exist, yet you don't. From what I have seen and are told you pop in and out of their lives at will. But remember this, if any harm comes to anyone in this family you will have me to hide from for the rest of your sorry life!

Then Bob did the strangest thing. He turned to John and lowered his sunglasses so John could see his scarred eyes were streaming tears, "For now I must ask you to trust I am doing the right thing old friend."

John suddenly thought he understood, "Well then let's enjoy the day with the Turner Family."

Just then they were pulling into the marina to launch the boat and enjoy the lake. The men launched the bass boat into the lake as Susan collected the picnic items and prepared them on one of the public tables. The boys grabbed their fishing rods and went in different directions to catch the biggest fish.

Crystal came walking up to Mike with her little Snoopy Rod in hand, "Daddy, I want to fish too!"

Mike took a minnow from the cooler and placed it on her hook.

"Daddy look, I caught one already!"

Everyone laughed as Mike explained, "Honey, it's only the minnow you will use to catch a fish."

"But Daddy, it looks like a fish."

Mike couldn't feel more proud of his little girl.

"I know sweetheart, but let's just say we're going to make a little deal with God." Mike kneeled down before her.

"We're going to offer Him this little fish for a bigger fish and see if He will take our offering."

She looked at her dad in shock, "I thought the preacher said we weren't supposed to tempt God the other Sunday, Daddy."

Susan jumped in, "Yeah Mike, how are you going to explain this one?"

They all laughed as Mike again tried to explain. "Well honey, we're not tempting Him we're just asking Him to give us a larger fish that will be able to feed our family if He sees fit to do so. Don't you remember the story of Jesus who feed the multitude with only a few fish and a loaf of bread?"

Crystal smiled, "You mean sort of like when Jesus took a few fish and fed everyone."

"Yes honey, that's right. We just want enough to try and feed everyone."

"But Daddy, we don't need a whole lot of fish like Jesus did. This would be wasteful and I don't think I can eat very many!"

Mike knew when he was beat, "Yes honey, you're right. Now go over there and put the minnow in the lake and see if you catch a bigger fish, maybe just one or two."

Everyone was having a good time. Crystal and Willy didn't fish very long as usual and wanted to go swimming. So Susan and the kids went swimming in the lake while the men went off in the boat to try and catch a few bass.

Mike noticed John appeared to be especially happy for some reason, "It appears you don't go fishing much. You look like a kid who's going for the first time."

John laughed out loud, "No I enjoy fishing when I can. I just don't get to go much. I suppose I'm enjoying the company more than the trip. Guess I'd forgotten how much fun it can be on a family outing such as this."

Bob looked at John, "Couldn't have said it any better myself."

All good things have an ending, and the family outing was no exception to the rule. Too soon it seemed they were leaving and headed back home to Montgomery.

"Are you sure you don't want to stay and go back Monday, John. We'd be glad to have you and are welcome to stay and attend Church with us tomorrow."

"I do appreciate it, but I need to get Mary's car back to her. I really enjoyed the day and maybe we can do it again real soon."

John and Bob walked out to the car and Bob shook hands again with John. They talked for a minute then John got in the car and left.

Mike asked Bob, "How do you like John?"

Bob smiled, "Like I've known him all my life. He certainly seems to be a very good friend to you and your family."

"How was the trip up from Montgomery?" asked John.

"Not too bad, just got a little sore riding in my little truck. It doesn't ride very good at all."

"I think Mary has a truck ready for you. Let's go see."

They walked inside through dispatch then into Mary's office and sat down.

Mary looked at them and remarked, "You two look bright eyed and bushy tailed this morning. What's going on with you?"

John said, "You sure do look pretty this morning. What did you do, have your hair done or something?"

"Okay, now I know something's up. Now what is it?"

Mike looked around the room, "There's nothing I know anything about."

Mary looked back at John. John looked down.

"Nothing's wrong. We just had a good weekend and I wish you could have been there too. I believe you would have enjoyed it, Ms. Mary."

"Well no one invited me. I'm not one to go where I'm not wanted," as Mary pretended to feel slighted.

Mike jumped in and explained, “Ma'am, we're sorry. We didn't realize you may have wanted to go. I'm ashamed to admit I didn't even think about it. Even after John said he was going to borrow one of your cars I should’ve thought to invite you. I am sorry.”

Mary laughed, “I'm just picking at you. I already had plans for the weekend. And there you go with the ma’am crap again!”

“Sorry again, Ms. Mary, it’s the way I was raised to respect all women.”

“Well I can see. Maybe it’s just me trying to hold on to my youth and deny elder respect for myself. I will try to make an exception for you, especially since you seem to be a good kid.”

“Thank you, Ms. Mary.”

“But you know I always did enjoy the little fishing trips Alan used to take me on and would love to do it again. Maybe that’s why I still hold on to his boat. It’s one of the few things I have left to remind me of him.”

Mike said, “Then the next time Bob's in town we'll be sure and ask you if you want to go.”

“I appreciate it, but who is Bob?”

John jumped in, “He's a friend of Mike and his family. I believe you would be impressed with him. He has a handicap, but he doesn't let it get him down. I sure like him.”

Mary glanced over at John scornfully, “Sounds as though you're trying to set me up, John. Now what did I tell you the last time you tried this?”

“Mary, I know full well what you said. There was only one man in this life for you and he is gone. But it doesn't mean you can't at least enjoy life. Maybe even find another friend to enjoy life with.”

“Okay we'll talk about this some other time. For now we have to get this driver in his own truck.”

She looked at the list of trucks and assigned Mike one of the newest she had available at the moment. Then Mike and John walked back out onto the yard to see his new truck.

As John and Mike walked across the yard Mike asked, “Who is Alan?”

John snickered, “It’s Hammer’s first name. We all called him Hammer, but Mary insisted on calling him by his first name, Alan. Mary doesn’t think CB handles are appropriate!”

The truck Mike was assigned appeared to be well maintained. He could find nothing in need of repair and it was even very clean. Mike knew there could always be little things would show up in time, but as for now it appeared to be reliable enough to take a load and go on a trip. John suggested he take a short run to begin with just in case. Mike walked in the office and asked dispatch what they had for him. He was offered loads going out to Texas, but decided to take one to Mobile instead. His reason was twofold. One, it was short and would allow him to get used the truck and the second reason was he could go by the house and give his little girl a ride in daddy's new truck. So Mike went to the steel mill and loaded for Mobile.

It was late afternoon when Mike pulled into his driveway with the new truck. Everyone ran outside to see it and after loading them up they went for a short ride down the road. Soon it was time to leave and get on down to Mobile. As Mike made it out to Interstate 65 and got started south he realized it was the actual beginning of his trucking career and he would remember this for the rest of his life. He came up on another flat bed and started talking to him on the CB. Turned out he was going to the same place Mike was and knew how to get there. Mike decided to run along with him to Mobile. Somehow this would make it better than being alone. Seemingly before he knew it they were in Mobile.

It didn't take long to get unloaded at the steel supply house and soon Mike was calling to get his next dispatch. Dispatch sent him to the Alabama State docks to pick up a load for Nashville. It happened the other flatbed driver was going to the docks as well and could help Mike with the procedures there. Mike never knew there were so many hoops to jump through just to get on the docks to load. Once there he had more government red tape to navigate to get loaded. He thought, why so darn much security and meaningless paperwork? Eventually he was loaded and on his way. He stopped at his home in Montgomery and ate a late dinner with the family and soon was off to Nashville for delivery. He thought, so far so good.

He had a hard time finding the place in Nashville even after calling and getting directions. Mike soon learned there are some people in this world who simply cannot tell you how to get to where they are and never will. Even though they may have lived in a place all their lives they simply don't know where they are in relation to somewhere else. When he finally got there he was in the middle of town and was not seeing what he expected to in downtown Nashville.

There were bums and hookers all around. Also run down warehouse buildings along with dilapidated business buildings everywhere. He could only wonder what the percentages were for the ones who ran away from home to “Music City” in hopes of making it big. How many out of a hundred made it? How many didn't? How many went back home? And just how many never got the chance to go back home? But rather stayed here in the hobo jungle of old forgotten buildings. At one time these people were someone's pride and joy brought into this world with such high hopes. What happened and where did things go wrong? Mike always believed there was a reason for everything in life that happened, either human or divine. He had a hard time believing God would turn his back on them, but believed the reverse could be the case. Whatever each unique case may be they were here now and all of them had one unmistakable thing in common, hopelessness.

Where the rest of the world lived with the notion what I will do this weekend or next holiday or next vacation, these people were more concerned with the next hour. And if they happened to awake the next morning, the next night was in question. Yes, these were the forgotten and the overlooked which only by the Grace of God could be anyone of us. Mike looked around one last time before leaving going back to Birmingham and load the next day. This is one of the things a truck driver sees on a regular basis. Would there perhaps be some changes made if the entire world was forced to see it on a daily basis? Or would everyone simply ignore it as most of the people who live near do? Mike put it in gear, let out on the clutch and put it behind him for now.

"You got a load?" asked John as he roused Mike.

Mike looked out the driver's side window sleepy eyed. "Not yet. What time is it?"

"About 6:00. You intend to sleep all day kid?"

Mike grinned, "I did intend to sleep until they got to work at the office."

"Get on up. I'm ready for some breakfast. We'll take your pickup truck."

Mike climbed down and they got in his little truck to head for the restaurant. Niki's was one of the more famous of the eateries in town. Good food served cafeteria style and priced reasonable. Mike and John were enjoying breakfast when some of the drivers came in. John called to them and they came and sat close to John and Mike. John introduced them to Mike and then they all started exchanging stories as will happen with a group of drivers. There were stories and tall tales you would probably need to take with a grain of salt and then others were quite comical. Of course John had to tell everyone about Mike and his daughter, Crystal, arguing over whether her minnow was in fact a fish. Soon it was time to leave, go back to dispatch and see what the day would bring. On the way back Mike made the statement the drivers he met appeared to be good people.

John agreed, “Not a one in the bunch I wouldn't trust my life to. If there are a better bunch of drivers around I don’t know them.”

They pulled onto the yard and got out. Mike said, “Guess it's time to see what they have in store for us,” as they walked into dispatch.

“Do you have two of them?” John asked the dispatcher when offered a load to Saint Louis.

“Yeah, but how are you going to pull two of them with one truck?”

John laughed then turned to Mike, “You want to go with me to Saint Louis, Mike?”

“Sure, should be able to load back fairly easy, shouldn't we?”

The dispatcher set them both up with loads of pipe to “The Gate Way”. They went to the cast iron pipe yard and took their spot in line with the other drivers. They found the loads were going to a job site which meant there were probably multiple loads and could take quite a while to get unloaded. It was too late since they were already committed to loading them. They would have to make the best of it when they got there. Finally they got out of the pipe yard a little after noon and would have to hurry to get there by tomorrow. Soon they were on their way north on Interstate 65 toward Nashville.

Mike called out to John on the CB radio, “I'm really starting to get to know this stretch of road here. This is the second time this week I've been through here.”

“I'm afraid you'll get more familiar with it,” replied John.

"That is when you're driving out of Birmingham, Rookie."

"Yeah, I can see that!"

They were in Tennessee close to the Tennessean truck stop when Mike noticed the billboard for the truck stop. "John, is the food any good at the Tennessean?"

"Yeah, usually is. Why, are you getting hungry, Rookie?"

"A little, I'm mostly kind of sore and a little weak. Think I may need something in my stomach."

So they stopped and went inside. Mike went to the restroom and went into one of the stalls to get some toilet tissue to blow his nose. When he did he noticed a little blood on the paper. He thought how strange, he didn't feel as though he were coming down with a cold or anything. He figured it could be lack of sleep. He went into the restaurant sat down and ordered. While sitting there he began to feel a little dizzy. Soon the food came and he slowly ate his meal. He sat back and sipped on his coffee while he waited on John to finish his dessert.

Concerned, John watched Mike for a moment. "Do you feel any better now?"

Mike nodded his head. "I think I was just a little tired and hungry. It could be because someone woke me up too dad burn early this morning!"

"Let's get on up the road and maybe you'll get some sleep tonight." They continued their journey for Saint Louis. The 76 truck stop in Mount Vernon, Illinois was a little crowded when they got there. However, they did manage to find a couple of spots to park.

John got out of his truck and walked over to Mike's.

"Think I'm going inside, Rookie. I need a grilled cheese and some milk before bed. Are you going inside too?"

Mike shook his head, "I'm not feeling too well. I believe I need to go on to bed and get some rest. Just wake me up in the morning when you're ready."

John agreed then left to go inside to the restaurant.

As he walked across the lot he thought I sure hope he's not getting sick. He's been out of work quite a while. I don't think his family needs this now. No matter who you are being sick can be hard to deal with. But when you drive a truck for a living it's almost unbearable! Everything will get to you such as traffic or people at the businesses and even the weather. The problem is you can't take the day off and go home to someone who cares and would be sympathetic to your feelings. Instead you have exactly the opposite on the road.

The next morning John woke Mike and told him come inside for breakfast. John was already on his second cup of coffee when Mike stumbled into the restaurant.

John looked at him, "Boy, you look like death warmed over. You must not feel any better."

Mike yawned, "No, I feel alright at the moment. I could have used some more sleep, but we have to go on and get unloaded. Is the food any good here?"

John just nodded, "I like the western omelets here, but you decide what you want, it's all good."

Mike ordered an omelet and coffee.

John took a closer look at Mike and remarked again, "You really don't look so good, are you sure you're okay?"

Mike sighed, "I'd be telling a lie if I said I felt the best I ever have, but I think it's from a lack of sleep. While I was off all I did was sleep. Guess I've yet to get back into a routine."

"I don't know you really look pale to me. But if you say you're alright then I guess you are."

John was really starting to get concerned.

They got to the job site a little late and had a few trucks ahead of them in line. It was a little after 1:00 in the afternoon when they finally got unloaded and were told it would be tomorrow before they would get another load. So they decided to go back across the River to the Skelly Truck Stop in East St. Louis, Illinois to spend the night.

It was Mike's first time in the Skelly and not impressed with the crowded situation when they pulled onto the lot. It was starting to look as though they were not going to find a place to park, but after riding around a while they finally found a couple of places in the back lot. John and Mike were walking up to the restaurant when a woman stopped them and asked for a cigarette. John was the only one who smoked so he gave her a cigarette and then a light. They started to walk on when the woman stopped them again and asked for money to get something to eat. John gave her a five dollar bill and they went on into the truck stop.

Mike was first to make a remark, "The whole time this was going on I kept thinking of the rip off by the man in Florida the other day."

"Yeah, I can see it. Actually I figured at some point she was going to offer sex for money. But I have to say she wasn't exactly a raving beauty."

"It appears to me trucking sure attracts the worst in life for some reason."

Mike and John walked into the restaurant and sat down. They looked at the menu and ordered dinner. Mike looked around the restaurant at the unique decor. It appeared to him to be from the late 50s or early 60s.

"How old is this place?"

"Not sure Rookie, it's been here longer than I've been driving is all I can say."

They finished eating, paid their tickets and then went to the driver's lounge to check out the television. It was so crowded all they could do was stand around trying to get a glance at the TV since all the chairs were occupied. While John stood at the door Mike told him he was going to find a phone and call home.

Mike went to the pay phones and made his usual person to person call leaving a message with the number to the pay phone he was on. He was standing by the phone waiting when another driver asked to use the phone. It appeared he was going to have some strong words with the man when Susan called him back. The man went to another phone.

"How are you doing, darling?" Susan asked.

"I feel a little sore and tired, but otherwise not too bad. He held back the episode about the bloody nose and fatigue.

"Where are you at tonight? And you better not be with one of the girls!"

Mike laughed, "Of course not since there's only one woman for me and I have enough trouble keeping up with her. John and I are in East St. Louis, Illinois at a truck stop. We unloaded today and have to wait until tomorrow for a load. How is everything going at home?"

"Everything's fine. How did you and John wind up together?"

"Dispatch happened to have two of these loads so I took one along with John to get a little more experience in this area."

They talked a little more and Mike talked to his children. It was good to hear their voices even though it had only been a couple of days since last seeing them. After ending his conversation with home Mike found John and informed him he was going to call it a night. John told him to get plenty of rest because tomorrow could be a very long day.

John finally found a seat in the driver's room to watch the TV. Of course when you have such a large group of people there is always one who simply can't be quiet. John left for bed.

The next morning John decided to let Mike sleep long as possible. He didn't think it was lack of sleep causing Mike to feel so bad, but just in case he'd let him get plenty of rest.

John went inside and called dispatch to check in and see if there were any loads. He was told it was early yet and dispatch would page him at the truck stop. John sat down in the restaurant and ordered breakfast. He was starting to sense it could be a long wait for a load. He looked around the restaurant and recognized several drivers he knew pulled flat beds realizing they too were probably waiting for a load from the steel mill. He looked out the window and observed it was now raining. This could put a damper on things also. Since most loads from the mill had to be covered out of the weather, the time needed for loading would increase dramatically. Yes, it was shaping up to be one of those days for sure. The waitress asked if he needed more coffee.

"May as well, can't dance."

"You must be from the South, what part?"

"I'm from Birmingham, although I don't have a home there or anywhere in fact. It just seems to be where I spend most of my off time."

"If you only knew how many times I've heard this story," the waitress said skeptically. "I'll bet you have a wife, six kids and a mortgage big as Texas. In fact, you're just looking for a girl to feel sorry for you and get fooled into messing around with you," as she stood and smiled at him.

John quickly got angry and then realized she was probably right in most cases. He had seen it also.

"No ma'am, just stating a fact to you. You can believe it or not, doesn't matter to me. You asked me a question, I gave you an answer. I don't know you so I will accept the things you tell me are true until or if proven wrong. I would appreciate the same from you."

She nodded her head and refilled his coffee cup then went to help her other customers. John thought and contemplated she may have proven a point she didn't even know about John. It could be the reason he was still alone this late in life was not so much finding the right woman, but finding himself instead.

He thought how quickly he got mad at her and how ridiculous it was for him to make the statement he did. Perhaps he would never find *Miss Right* until he stopped proving to every woman he met he was *Mr. Wrong*. It was about then Mike came walking into the restaurant.

John quickly came back to the moment, “How do you feel this morning?”

Mike stretched and yawned, “I feel a little better now. Why didn't you wake me up before you came in here?”

“I just wanted to let you rest as much as you could. In fact after you eat you may as well go lay back down if you want. There's not much going on, the rain will make it even slower.”

The waitress came over and asked for Mike's order.

“Give me a minute to wake up and look the menu over.”

The waitress nodded then walked off. Mike looked the menu over then decided to wait and get lunch a little later.

He glanced at the waitress then winked at John. “She seems nice and she's definitely pretty. Be a good day to get to know her.”

“You’re barking up the wrong tree son. That squirrel's already gone.”

Puzzled, Mike looked at John, “Huh?”

“Never mind, not important, sure you don't need to eat now? It may make you feel better.”

“I think I'll do what you suggested, go lay down and rest some more. I just wish I knew what was making me feel so bad. I get to feeling better and then all of a sudden I will get weak again.”

The waitress came back over and asked for his order again.

Mike explained he just wanted some coffee for now.

He sat and sipped some coffee. “When do you think we'll get a load John?”

John sipped some of his coffee then answered.

"I'm not sure. It could be late today or may even be tomorrow before we get out of here. These things happen and you just have to grin and bear it."

"I'm going to the truck. Come get me if something happens." Mike got up and went outside.

John was in the driver's room watching TV when the page came over the intercom for Mike or him. He went to the phone and answered the page from dispatch. They told him there would be two loads going back to Birmingham at the steel mill the next morning. He got all the information he needed and ended the call. He thought a minute and decided to let Mike rest for now. He would wake him up a little later to eat and tell him about the loads. He went back to the driver's room and continued to watch the TV although it was a little tough to do with all the drivers talking and telling stories and such. It was just a typical rainy day.

The next morning John awakened Mike. He told him they would meet inside the restaurant. John was sitting at the table sipping coffee as Mike came walking in.

As Mike started to sit down he stopped and told John, "I left my billfold in the truck. I'll be right back."

"You don't have to go back, I'll pay for your meal and you can pay me back later."

Mike told John he appreciated it, but he needed to go get his billfold anyway. Mike started out to his truck when a young man stopped him inside the truck stop.

"You know much about this area?"

Mike told him no, what was he looking for? The man told him he was looking for a certain business was supposed to be around there. Mike said he couldn't help him, but maybe they would know at the fuel desk. When Mike started to walk away the man again jumped in front of him and asked if he had been driving long? Mike thought it was an odd question, but told him he had been driving for a little while now. Mike started for his truck and again the man jumped in front of him asking another silly question. Mike simply told him he had to go to the truck now since his partner was waiting on him. He was sorry, but he had to go. The man moved and let Mike go. Mike thought about it and wondered what was up with the man. He came back to the table and told John what happened.

John took on a worried look. “Was your truck alright? Did you see where anyone tried to break into it?”

Mike looked startled. “No, why would you say that?”

John explained sometimes thieves would watch and when you went into the truck stop to eat or whatever they would break into your truck. Sometimes they would have a partner inside to watch and if you were to start back too soon they would try to delay you.

“I didn't see anything wrong, but we'll look a little closer when we go back.”

They ordered their meals. After finishing breakfast they went to their trucks to get ready to load. Mike went to his truck first and opened the door to look around. Mike called out to John and said he didn't see any problems inside the truck. John walked around to the passenger side of the truck and called for Mike to come outside where he was.

Mike walked around the front of the truck. “What's wrong over here, John?”

When Mike got around the truck to the passenger side he could see what was wrong. “Darn,” exclaimed Mike, “they stole my fuel!”

John stood there and shook his head. “They always steal it from the passenger side for two reasons.”

It's pretty well known most drivers sleep with their heads on the driver’s side of the truck. Also the fuel gauge is always in the driver's side tank. If you happen to be asleep in the truck you will be less apt to hear them stealing your fuel from the opposite side of the truck. If they drain the right side tank, it will take an hour or more for the fuel to equalize from left to right and reflect the new fuel level. This means you would be several miles up the road before you knew someone had stolen fuel from you and they would be long gone.

Mike stood and shook his head at what he was seeing. The fuel cap was still off and there was a fuel soaked rag on the ground along with the strong smell of spilled fuel everywhere. His tanks were not far from being full and each tank held around a hundred and twenty gallons of fuel, meaning the thieves stole around one hundred gallons. Mike could only stand and shake his head some more. This was just beyond belief for him.

As expected there was a long line of trucks at the steel mill waiting to get loaded. John and Mike were thankful it was not raining, at least and they wouldn't get wet covering the load. Mary was not happy to hear about the fuel getting stolen, but she knew how life on the road can be so she didn't make a big fuss over it. Mike was told to fuel up at the Skelly and forget about it for now. Things went fairly fast and they were loaded quicker than anticipated. They were on their way south to Birmingham and none too soon far as Mike was concerned. It had been a long, tough week and he was ready to get home to his family.

"How far do you feel like going?" asked John.

"We'll see what happens. Right now I believe I can go all the way."

"So you feel good now?"

"Yeah, I feel alright, don't seem to have any problems to speak of. No fatigue or dizziness. Let's go home."

"You better tighten up and come on," John yelled on the CB.

"I'm getting tired of waiting on you," cried John impatiently.

Mike picked up the microphone. "I'm peddling as fast as I can back here. I'll catch up to you shortly."

They were just getting to the Alabama State line and it seemed the trip was getting longer and longer. Mike felt as though they were never going to get to Birmingham. Mike wasn't going to tell John, but he was starting to feel really bad now and it was coming on fast. But he was determined to get back home before anyone knew about it. He simply had to make it back home. As they pulled onto the yard in Birmingham Mike was so glad to have this much done. Now if only he could just get to Montgomery.

John got out of his truck and walked over to Mike's. "We made it to Birmingham. Guess you can go home and come back Monday to unload."

"Yeah, it's going to be a long ride home as tired as I am right now, but I'll get there."

"Be careful going home, I'll see you Monday."

Mike got into his pickup. "You have a good weekend too. See you later."

Mike slowly pulled from the yard and headed toward home.

By the time Mike got to Montgomery he was delirious from the fever and Susan couldn't believe he drove home in such a condition. "Why didn't you call me? I would have come gotten you, Mike. And John would have brought you home also. You better not ever do this again!"

At this point she may as well have been talking to the wall. Mike collapsed on the bedroom floor, but he was home with his family and now felt safe and at ease.

Hammer Lane Express

Chapter Six

Reunion

The doctor came into the hospital room and shook hands with Mike, then Susan.

"I told you to tell me if you had anymore weak spells or dizzy spells, Mike. So what happened?"

Mike looked sheepishly at the doctor. "I was simply trying to get home. I didn't want to be in the hospital on the road. I know you would have told me go to an emergency room somewhere, now wouldn't you?"

"I wouldn't want you to take a chance and have a wreck, maybe kill yourself or someone else."

But that's beside the point now. We need to find out what's causing all this trouble for you. I've scheduled some tests for this evening and hopefully we'll find out what this is. For now I need you to stay calm and don't give the nurses or your wife a hard time. You're too young to be having these kinds of problems and it has me puzzled as to the cause. It may take a little while, but we fully intend to get to the bottom of it.

Susan nervously questioned, "What do you think it is doctor? Does it have anything to do with his ribs getting injured when he fell off the load in Little Rock?"

"I don't think so," answered the doctor, "this appears to have been going on earlier."

Although it's something we can't be sure of until we get the test results and plot a course of action for treatment. He paused a moment, let's be clear about something. Mike comes into the emergency room with a fever of a hundred and four, incoherent and rambling on about someone stealing fuel wanting somebody to call the police plus as pale as a sheet. Am I concerned about his prognosis? Of course I am! And you should be too. We're not going to stop until we know what's wrong here.

"Thank you doctor, keep us informed, please." said Susan.

The doctor smiled and nodded his head then walked out.

John was just getting back to the yard when he heard, "Big John, come to the office, please," over the yard intercom. He parked his truck and went inside. Mary met him at her office door.

"John, come inside a moment, please."

He walked inside and she closed the door. She sat down and looked up at John. "Mike's in the hospital in Montgomery. They don't know what's wrong with him and he's been in there since Saturday morning."

"Why didn't he say something when we got here Saturday? I would have taken him to the hospital, or to Montgomery or wherever he wanted."

Mary smiled and explained, "No one's blaming you for anything, John. We all know you would've done anything needed. I do need to ask you if you will go and deliver Mike's load for him, please if you don't mind."

John nodded his head. "Keep me informed on his condition."

Mary agreed, “By the way, John, the new trainee will be ready today if you want to take him on. I'll understand if you don't, it's up to you.”

John thought a moment. “We better get him in here or we may lose him same as the last.”

Mary again agreed telling John she would handle it. John went and climbed in Mike's truck and went to deliver the load he brought in.

The Susan answered the phone in Mike’s room. “How's Mike doing?” inquired Bob.

“He's sleeping for now.”

They have him on some strong a medications at the moment which keep him in and out. They have more tests to run this afternoon and even more for tomorrow morning. Hopefully we'll find out soon what's wrong, but for now it's anyone's guess.

Bob told her he would be calling every day to check on him. When Bob hung up the phone it immediately rang again. This time it was John, “How's Mike?”

Again Susan explained what was going on.

“Is there anything I can do or help with?”

“We do appreciate you, but we're okay for now. Just stay in touch.”

John ended the call on the pay phone in the driver's room. Then John walked into the office where Mary introduced his new trainee to him.

“John, this is Mark Albertson. Mark, this is John and if he wants you to know his last name he'll tell you.”

They shook hands. “So you think you're ready to go?” asked John.

“I hope so. I've been out of work for too long already.”

John looked at him closer. Mark appeared to be very young.

"You look really young. Just how old are you?"

"What did you say your last name was?"

"Be here early tomorrow, ready to go and don't be late. I WILL leave without you!"

"How early is early?"

"If when you get here you don't see me or the truck sitting there, you can go back home cause you were too late. Understood?"

Mark nodded his head and walked off.

John turned to Mary, "Feisty little man, huh?"

Mary laughed. "May have met your match this time hand," and walked out to dispatch.

John hated it when Mary used the old term hand as in what was referred to as a farm or ranch worker. It was short for hired hand and she often didn't mean it in a respectful manner. It was a term truckers still use today, but in Mary's case it probably came from her North Texas/South Oklahoma family roots. He often wondered if she may be related to the famous outlaw of the area, Black Jack Ketchum since it was her maiden name.

Susan was beginning to feel like Mike's secretary rather than his wife, every time she turned around the phone was ringing. Family members and friends were continually calling to check on him. She was glad to have so many people who cared. But it could be quite an inconvenience since every time she wanted to go to the restroom, get a cup of coffee or eat it seemed the phone would ring. The orderlies came in to get Mike for tests and said they would be back in about an hour. Susan decided it would be a good time to go and eat. She went downstairs to the cafeteria and went through the line getting a few vegetables plus a piece of chicken and of course, coffee. She sat down and began to eat. As she cut her food up into bites she noticed her hands start to shake a little. When she was about to put a bite into her mouth her right hand suddenly began shaking violently as she spilled the food back onto the plate. She could hold back the tears no longer. She could pretend everything would be alright no further. Susan was unable to project the pretense she was a super woman who could handle anything to come down the road. Her sweetheart, soul mate and friend for life was having tests done trying to determine what was trying to take him away from her. It was the first time since the ordeal started she was alone and had to face her fears. She sat and quietly sobbed.

"Mrs. Turner?" asked the candy stripe volunteer.

"Yes."

"Your husband is back in his room and asking for you."

Susan wiped the tears back, "The big baby can't even survive one minute without my help."

She got up and put her tray away. The little volunteer grabbed Susan's arm as they walked back to the elevator. "You know you're not alone. We are all here to help with whatever you need. For anything we can't help with we have a hospital Chaplain to ease your troubled mind if you like."

"I know honey," replied Susan. "Believe it or not I was once a candy striper too."

In fact, it's how I met my husband, Mike. You see his parents were in a terrible car accident. His mom was killed immediately and his dad lingered for over two weeks before God took him home. I was a volunteer here and tried to help his family the best I could. His brother and sister took it very hard. But Mike being the oldest seemed to take it the hardest of all. God seems to put the people we need most in our lives before us when we least expect it as you are here now. Don't forget that.

"Yes ma'am," responded the young lady.

Susan walked into the hospital room and smiled at Mike. He smiled back as she ran to hold him. He was hers for now and for now was all she needed.

It was late the next morning when the doctor came in to see Mike and Susan. As usual he shook Mike's hand, then Susan's.

"We haven't gotten all the results from the tests back yet, but so far so good."

We have ruled out some of the more serious ailments so far and remain cautiously optimistic until we get the other results. We have a few more tests to do today and will get a better idea of where to go from there perhaps tomorrow. Do you have any questions at this time for me?

Mike shook his head no and Susan asked, "Is there anything we should be doing?"

"Not at this time," remarked the doctor. "Just keep him calm and make him rest. Okay, I'll get back with you tomorrow."

The doctor patted Mike on the back and left.

Susan hugged her husband, "Honey, it's not going to be so bad. They're going to get you better in no time at all."

Mike smiled then looked into his wife's eyes, "You always knew how to cheer me up when things were so bad I didn't want to go on. I do thank God for you!"

John took a long look at the clothes and gear Mark had in his car. "Are you sure there wasn't anything else you could have bought from home, rookie?"

Mark quickly turned around to John, "I don't have a home other than this car here. I lost my apartment two weeks ago and have been living out of this car ever since."

"Sorry, I didn't know. Why didn't you let Ms. Mary know? She would have done something to get you by. It wasn't your fault we couldn't get you into the program until now."

"I didn't see it as her problem, but rather mine."

I'm the one who decided to leave home and go back to school. I'm the one who quit my old job and made this career change. No one forced me into this as I decided it on my own.

John informed Mark, "We only have limited room for gear in the truck. You need to decide what you absolutely need and leave the rest. Don't worry about what's left in the car. We have a guard when everyone's gone and no one will break into your car."

Mark nodded then picked out what he needed and put it in the truck. Soon they were on their way to the steel mill to load for Chicago.

As they were sitting at the mill, Mark queried, "How long have you been driving, John?"

"I've been out here for a little over twenty years now."

"Have you ever wished you never started?"

"I regret it every single day, rookie."

Mark shook his head then commented, "That's very encouraging!"

In his usual cheerful manner John replied, "Yep!" Then it was their turn to load.

"Are you ready to drive, rookie?" asked John.

"That's why I'm here."

John put his gloves up and climbed in on the passenger side. Mark climbed in on the driver's side and adjusted the seat since he was quite a bit shorter than John.

"You need something to sit on?"

Mark looked over at John and gave him a go to Hell look as he continued to adjust the seat. Once he was adjusted Mark put the truck in gear and started off. He had a little trouble with the gears at first, but soon settled down and was back on the interstate. He didn't get very far until the interstate ended and he had to get off and go through Fultondale.

"I thought Interstate 65 went all the way up to Chicago."

"It does."

"Then why do we have to get off here and go through town?"

"Interstate 65 is not yet completed through here," said John.

"I don't know why it's not. But for now we have to go around. I can't believe you haven't been up here before. Don't you live here in town?"

"No, I lived in Tuscaloosa most of my life."

"We have just a few miles and we will be back on the interstate. Just look at it this way, you will get a little more practice shifting gears at all these red lights."

"I don't need any practice at shifting gears!"

"As I said, you can use this time to get a little more practice at shifting gears, rookie," as he took a long, hard look at Mark.

"Whatever!" Mark mumbled.

The phone rang again and Susan answered, "Hello."

"How is Mike doing now?" asked Mary

"He's still sleeping for now, Ms. Mary. He's still on the high strength medications and is in and out most of the time. How are you doing?"

Mary was shocked Susan would ask about her at a time like this. "I'm doing fine. John has a new trainee with him now. In fact they left a while ago to load for Chicago. Is there anything I can do for you?"

"Not at the moment, just pray for us is all."

Mary informed Susan the whole office had been praying for them and would continue to do so.

"Please tell everyone how much we appreciate them and thank them for us." Mary told her she would.

Then the phone rang again and Susan answered.

Bob asked, "Hey Susan, how's Mike doing today?"

"He's still sleeping as usual."

"Has the doctor said anything yet?"

"Only some of the test results came back negative and he was cautiously optimistic right now. They took him for some more tests today and we probably won't hear more until tomorrow."

"Is there anything else I can do for you? I'm in Atlanta now and can come your way if you need me."

"No, but I do appreciate you. Just keep in touch and go on about your business. Hopefully tomorrow we might know a little more."

Bob said he would call her later and ended the call.

"Good morning," said the doctor as he walked into the room.

Susan and Mike both answered, "Good morning," back to him.

He stood by the bed and looked at Mike. "I haven't gotten all the results back, but so far we have yet to find anything to be concerned with. You appear to be responding to the antibiotics now and your white cell count is going down. I do want to check something one of my colleagues mentioned this morning as I was discussing your case with him."

He bent over and asked Mike to open his mouth. He looked inside Mike's mouth and pulled Mike's cheek back as he glanced at his gums. He then took a light and shined back in Mike's throat. He stood back looking at Mike in deep thought as he rubbed his own chin. "Would you mind if I let another doctor come and take a look at you?"

"No, but why do you want to have another doctor take a look?"

"Sometimes a fresh set of eyes can find what everyone else might be missing."

Susan told the doctor, "We're all for whatever it takes to get him well, go for it."

"It may be late today before he comes in. Now don't be alarmed, but he's an oncologist or a specialist in cancers. I'm not saying you have any signs of a cancer, Mike. I just want to rule it out, is that understood?"

Mike and Susan looked at each other and nodded back at the doctor.

"Good, he'll be in sometime today unless the test results come back this morning showing the cause of your problems. Until then rest and relax, Mike."

Then the doctor left. Mike and Susan looked at each other for a while. Then she grabbed him and they hugged for a very long time.

Susan confessed to Mike, "I can't help but worry until we find out what this is. I've prayed and prayed with everything I have in my soul. Maybe it's the woman in me, but I am so scared I may lose you I can't think straight."

Mike slowly rubbed on her arm and shoulder and with tears in his eyes, "I have to admit it scares me too."

It seems as though the not knowing is worse than the disease I must have. How can you fight the unknown? Let there be no doubt our belief in God will get us through this. No matter what it may be, no matter where it may take us! God has always been there for us through good times and bad. He will not let us down now regardless of the outcome. You are a strong God loving woman, Susan. Even though it should be my time to leave this world for a better one His will be done, I'm okay with knowing this. As God loves me I know I have been loved here on earth by you and the kids and would never be forgotten. I am at peace believing this as you should be too.

Mark and John took a little nap at the 76 in Gary, Indiana waiting for the customer to open so they could get directions to them. Mark was in the sleeper while John laid his head over the wheel. John shook Mark and told him to get ready. It was time for them to go inside and get some breakfast. It was starting to get daylight and as they were getting out they heard three quick gun shots which appeared to be very close.

Mark jumped. "What the Hell was that? Sounded like gunshots!"

John calmly responded, "It was."

"What are we going to do?"

"Do you see anyone with a gun running anywhere? Do you see anyone pointing a gun at you? Do you see anything at all?"

"No, what does it have to do with this?"

John calmly replied, "Then I suggest we go on about our business and continue to get breakfast."

Mark walked very close to John all the way to the restaurant. They sat down and Mark gawked at John.

"What?" John asked.

"Didn't that bother you at all back there?"

"If I were on the receiving end of the gun I would be very concerned. The fact is whoever or whatever the recipient of those three rounds was it's their business and not ours. I'm not going looking for them in the Chicago area. I'm just going on about my business."

Mark just couldn't seem to let it go. "What if it had been someone pointing a gun at us or after us?"

John calmly responded, "I suppose I would have gotten my Black Hawk out and blown them away."

Mark sat there in shock and was speechless. They finished breakfast then John called and got directions to the customer while Mark walked around the truck stop and looked at what was there. They went to the truck and left to deliver the load. It took a while to get unloaded and soon after they were John called dispatch to get the next load. He asked to speak to Mary before hanging up.

"Have you heard from Mike?" asked John.

"Not this morning," answered Mary. Then she added, "He was still sleeping and in and out yesterday when I talked to Susan. You can call back later and check if you want."

John said he'd call back later in the afternoon and see how he was doing.

Mark asked who John was talking about and John filled Mark in on Mike's situation. Mark said he hoped he would be alright. They went to a pipe yard and loaded oil field pipe for Tulsa. It took a while to get loaded and Mark wanted to know why it was taking so long?

"If you only knew how many times I've heard this question you wouldn't ask or expect an answer."

Mark scratched his head. "Are you trying to possibly tell me something?"

"Yeah, get used to it."

A couple of hours later they were loaded and had the load covered. John explained to Mark, "I'll drive out of town since its rush hour. When we get down the road somewhere I'll let you drive some more."

"You don't think I can handle Chicago rush hour traffic?"

"Let's just say I like living, rookie."

That afternoon an elderly gentleman in a long white coat came walking into Mike's room and introduced himself. He was a distinguished gentleman with snow white hair and a cheerful smile along with a unique mannerism. Just his presence seemed to relax Mike and Susan as though it were the Almighty himself or at the least one of His angels. They were in awe.

"Your doctor asked me to take a look at you and see what I thought might be wrong with you."

"Yes sir, he mentioned it to us this morning. He also said you were a cancer doctor."

"I specialize in treatment of some types of cancer, but that's not all I do. I also paint."

Mike asked, "Paint what?"

The doctor laughed, "Why pictures of course."

It's one of the hobbies I have I enjoy. You will see. He then took a look at Mike and asked him a few questions about his family.

"Do you have any brothers and sisters, Mike?"

"Yes sir, one brother and one sister."

"Has anyone in your family ever had any type of cancer?"

"No sir, I can't think of anyone."

"Good, that's good. How about your parents or grandparents, is there any cancer there?"

Mike swallowed hard. "My grandparents are just fine and have never had cancer to my knowledge. My parents were killed in a car wreck when I was eighteen."

The doctor smiled, "I am so sorry. Who finished raising you, your grandparents?"

"Yes sir, my brother, sister and I lived with them and I helped too. Since I was the oldest I went to work right out of high school and helped put them through school and into college."

"I see," said the doctor. "I'm going to order another test for you and then I'll be back with the results tomorrow evening."

He then turned and walked out.

Mike looked at Susan who was already looking at Mike with a puzzled expression. "What was all that about?"

Susan answered, "You're asking me? However, I like him. There's just something about him gives me confidence all will be well."

"I feel the same as you, Susan. Wonderful man it seems. All I can think is how blessed we are."

John stopped at the rest area just south of Chicago and let Mark take the wheel. "How far do you want me to drive?"

"Just don't forget to stop in Tulsa," as he leaned back into the seat and closed his eyes.

"Okay, Tulsa it is." As Mark let out the clutch and took off.

Traffic on Interstate 55 was about normal. It is one of the main routes to the southwest from Chicago and heavily traveled. Mark was getting his first experience in Illinois and enjoying the drive. He already had some experience with CB radios since he had been a member of a CB club in Tuscaloosa for years. He was driving along and talking to the other drivers and learning as he went he obviously didn't know quite as much about trucker talk on the CB as he thought he did. He soon turned the radio down and turned the FM radio on.

John woke up and told him, “Its country music or nothing!”

Mark protested, “I don't know anything about country music or even like it. I prefer rock myself.”

John told him, “That a fact?”

“Sure enough, I only like rock music.”

“That's nice. When you get your own truck you can burst your ear drums all you want. For now you'll put it on a country station or turn the damn thing off. Understood?”

Mark turned, looked at John then squawked, “Sure!”

Mark thought to himself this is going to be a very long trip. He couldn't help but wonder where he went wrong with John. He couldn't put his finger on it, but it appeared he had pissed John off somehow. To be perfectly honest he couldn't care less at the moment. He could hear John start to snore already and wondered how much of this he would be able to take.

It was about daylight when Bob pulled into the old 76 truck stop in Montgomery. He decided to take a nap and call Susan at the hospital a little later. There was simply no way he was going to stay away with Mike in the hospital. Especially when the doctors didn't know what was wrong with him. He went inside the truck stop restaurant with his sunglasses on as usual and sat down.

The waitress came over, began wiping the table and gawked.

"Let me guess. You must be a huge Ray Charles fan, driver."

Having heard it before Bob gave the same answer he had for years. "As a matter of fact I am. Would you like for me to wake him up so he can come in and greet you?"

Of course their answer was almost always the same. "Yeah right, now what can I get for you, driver?"

"Grilled cheese and milk will do me for now."

She smiled widely, "Trying to kill your dope, huh?"

"Something such as that. However, doesn't matter since I'm going to bed anyway. Care to join me?"

"Ha, in your dreams, driver!" she quickly replied.

The waitress brought his order to him and he sat back and ate his meal. He thought back on his life to this point and wondered where it would go from here. He thought about Mike, Susan and the kids. He considered himself lucky to be a part of their family and for them to be a major part of his life. He thought how strange life can be and how so many people can live their entire lives without knowing the peace he felt when he was spending time with the Turner family.

Susan was just coming back from getting breakfast and coffee in the cafeteria when she heard the phone ringing as she came into the room. Mike was sound asleep and not disturbed at all by the phone.

She picked up the phone as Bob surprised her, "Now surely you didn't think I could stay away did you?"

Susan giggled, "No guess I knew you'd be here as soon as possible. Where are you now?"

"I'm at the truck stop. I just woke up from a nap."

I've already called Mike's granddad and he's on his way to get me and take me to your house. I know where the spare key is and I'll take care of things at home, feed the pets and take care of them. Is there anything you need done at home before I come down to see Mike?

“I can't think of anything. Just do what you need to and when you come down I'll go back and take a shower and wash some clothes.”

“Okay, then I'll see you in a little while. How's he doing this morning?”

“He's sound asleep,” answered Susan. “I think he's doing alright at the moment.”

“I'll be there a little later. Don't worry, Susan. I'll take care of things at home for you.”

John stopped and called the customer to get directions at the 76 in Tulsa. Mark climbed out of the sleeper and went in with him. They got a couple of sausage biscuits and coffee to go then left to get unloaded. There were a few trucks ahead of them, but it didn't appear it would take long to get unloaded. They got out of the truck and started to prepare the load of pipe.

Mark asked, “Why does this pipe have so much oil on it?”

John looked at him, “To help keep it from rusting.”

“I can see that, but does it take this much oil? It seems like a waste to me.”

This is oil field drilling pipe. You see the threaded area inside of one end and the external treads on the other. They screw inside of each other and that's how they drill long distances. Each one of these is forty foot long and as they drill down they keep adding sections of this pipe to go deeper. These pipes here have been recycled or rebuilt to use again which means they have been processed to a point they will rust very fast. So they put sticky surface oil on them almost like STP oil treatment that will protect them better. Yes, it is aggravating to use your tarps on.

“But after a few loads and a little rain it will come off in time. Nothing actually last forever, it just seems to kid.”

"Then why are they putting it outside in the weather?"

John smirked, "They would have to pay someone to cover it here. They don't have to pay us to cover it on the truck."

Mark shook his head in disbelief and went on helping fold and roll up the tarps. Soon it was their turn to unload and John had Mark pull the truck up. Once they were empty they went back to the truck stop to call in and get lunch. John called for dispatch and was told to settle in since there was nothing there at the moment. John again asked for Mary and was told she was out and would be back after lunch. He hung up the courtesy phone at their table and looked over at Mark.

"They don't have anything for us now. I'll call back later and check with Ms. Mary. Have you decided what you want to eat?"

Mark was still looking at the menu then looked up, "Kind of hard to decide what I want."

It's starting to look like the same menu everywhere we go. Quarter fried chicken, half fried chicken, hamburger steak, chicken fried steak, BLT and none of it what I would consider to be reasonably priced. And the actual steaks, well I just want a piece of steak not the whole damn cow! I don't think I will ever make enough to buy a steak dinner here.

"I know. You may as well get used to it if you intend to hang with driving."

These truck stops know they have a captive audience and price everything accordingly. They know there are very few fast food places you can park anywhere near with an eighteen wheeler. If you are going to eat this is the only game in town.

The waitress asked if they were ready to order.

"Yeah, give me the chicken fried steak with fries and coffee," replied John.

She turned to Mark. "I will have the hamburger steak with mashed potatoes and gravy and coffee."

"Coming right up," she remarked and walked away.

Susan sat quietly in her chair. Bob should be there soon and relieve her long enough for her to go home to shower and wash her clothes. She thought it was a little late now and their doctor had yet to come in and see Mike. He was usually there early and now about two hours later than yesterday. Bob came walking in and she got up and hugged him. He looked over at Mike who was still asleep.

He then turned back to Susan. “How long has he been asleep?”

“He's been in and out ever since we've been here. I don't know what kind of antibiotics they have him on, but they do seem to put him out like a light.”

Bob thought a second then told Susan, “I don't think it's the antibiotics. They must have him on some type of pain pill or something. Was he having any pain when he came in?”

“He had no pain he was complaining about. He was just kind of out of it and rattling off about someone stealing his fuel. He wanted us to call the police because Mary simply wasn't going to believe him.”

Bob chuckled. “Yeah that would definitely get my attention. Gather up what you need washed and go on home. I'll stay with him and help keep an eye out while you're gone.”

“The doctor hasn't been in yet and I really don't want to leave until he comes in to tell us what he knows so far.”

“I know you want to stay, but I'm here and will ask the questions you and Mike won't. Go on and enjoy some home time. I'll see you later.”

Reluctantly she gathered up Mike's and her clothes and left. Bob sat down, picked up a magazine Susan was reading and settled in for what he knew would be a long day.

John and Mark had just gotten a load to pick up from dispatch. John was shocked it was actually in Tulsa. “I think this will be the first time ever I pick up a load here in Tulsa.”

John smiled, "I've been here many times, but always had to go way off somewhere to pick up."

"So I guess that's a good thing, huh?"

John looked hard at Mark, "When you get paid by the mile, you don't care how far you go to load."

But when you get paid a percentage of the revenue the empty miles are a freebie and you want to limit those best you can. No one likes to work for nothing and you soon will find there are way too many things in trucking you do for free. It's just part of this trucking life.

They pulled up to the steel supply house and went to check in. They were told to follow the drive around to the back and tell the men back there they were going to Birmingham. They did as they were told and the people in the back told them to stay in the truck until they came to get them since the load was not yet ready. They sat back and relaxed.

"You can lie down in the sleeper if you want and get some rest. You may start driving from here unless it doesn't take too long."

Mark climbed into the sleeper and stretched out to relax. It was about then John had a strange chill run up his spine and he got a sense something was wrong, but didn't know what.

Susan was in the middle of her shower when she felt a chill go through her like a bullet. She stopped, pulled the curtain back and looked around the room. There was nothing there so she continued with her shower. She just had a bad feeling and could not shake it. She climbed out and dried off with her towel and went to check on her clothes in the dryer. They were almost ready so she decided to fix a little something for a late lunch.

Then the phone rang and she answered it, "Hello."

Bob asked, "Is everything going okay at home, Susan?"

"Yes, I finished with my shower and fixed a sandwich to eat when you called. Is Mike alright?"

"He's asleep again, but he was awake for a short time earlier."

"I had the strangest chill go through me a while ago. It just had me worried."

Bob told her not to worry and when she was ready come on back. Susan hung the phone up and went to finish her meal.

Susan was just getting to the hospital when she felt the chill hit her again. She just didn't know what it could be, since it was almost ninety degrees outside and definitely not cold. She got out of the car and went inside. When she walked into the room the doctor who came in to see Mike the day before was standing by his bed. Bob was sitting in the chair looking down at the floor. Mike had a very faraway look in his eyes and his face was expressionless. The doctor turned around to Susan as Bob got up from the chair and had her sit down.

When Susan sat down the doctor explained the situation to her, "We got the test report back I had done yesterday and we now know what Mike's problem is."

Susan looked at everyone, "Am I to take it from the look on everyone's face the news will not be good?"

The doctor held her hand, "Mike has the beginning stages of leukemia and we're still trying to determine the exact stage he may have achieved."

Susan started to break down and cry as Bob went over to hold her. They hugged for a moment then Susan went and grabbed Mike and they hugged.

The doctor waited until he thought they were ready. "Now this is not always a terminal situation."

There are treatments available today we didn't have a year ago and advances are made every day. Leukemia is still a very deadly disease, but we have people today who have beaten it.

The first thing to do is to determine the stage and type and then start treatment for it. “Mike, you said you have a brother and a sister didn't you?”

“Yes sir, both are younger than me.” Mike then said, “Is this something they will need to be concerned about?”

“No, not at all,” said the doctor. “It’s possible we might need to do some testing on them if they agree to see if they may be a suitable donor if needed.”

“To see if they are suitable donors for what, doctor? I don't want them to go through life with missing parts, especially if it's just to prolong the inevitable.”

The doctor laughed. “No, what they may donate is a little bone marrow if needed which is nothing serious for them. But we have a lot of work to do until then. Get in touch with them and get them involved just in case.”

Bob, who was listening very intensely queried, “So doctor, you're saying in order to cure this Mike may need something from his relatives. Is this correct?”

“Yes and no,” explained the doctor. “What I mean is he may need a donation of bone marrow from a sibling and not a parent or cousin.”

I'm not saying someone other than this will not work. We have found so far a sibling's donation carries far less chance of rejection giving less chance of complications and will be more apt to work for Mike. It all depends on the type treatment we need to use to combat his illness and if his immune system is compromised. In some cases we may need the bone marrow to help Mike fight off further complications since certain treatments will destroy his immune system.

Bob’s facial expression was of total confusion. “Thank you doctor, please do all you can for him.”

The doctor nodded then told them, “I have more research to do and tests to run.” Then he turned and added information.

"Just in case start by getting in touch with your brother and sister and have each prepare for testing."

He then walked out of the room.

Bob, Susan and Mike all held hands and prayed. Susan told Mike all would be okay, we will beat this.

She then asked Bob, "Why the long face? It will be alright."

"I certainly hope and pray it will. We have much to consider."

John for some strange reason simply could not shake the feeling something wasn't right. He checked the load over and over, but could find nothing at all wrong with it. Everything was secured and ready to go.

Mark even asked, "Are we looking for something here or just what is the problem?"

John scratched his head and turned around. "No, I guess we're ready to go now. It just seems like we're missing something here."

Mark climbed in the driver's side as John got in the passenger seat and they were off. They headed down the turnpike toward Interstate 40. John explained how to get there to Mark and then laid back in the sleeper to rest awhile. Just before the interstate they came up on a fuel stop.

"Pull in here for a minute, rookie. I need to make a phone call."

Mark pulled in to the fuel stop and parked. They got out and went into the small seating area where there was a courtesy phone. John called the office and asked for Mary.

Soon she was on the line, "Have you heard anything from Mike today?"

Mary paused for a second, "Yes I have, just a little while ago. John, I'm afraid the news is not good."

John felt the chill again. "What do you mean, Ms. Mary? Do they know what's wrong with him now?"

“John,” answered Mary, “Mike has leukemia.”

“What is that and how will it affect Mike?”

“I'm not too sure what it is, but I do know it's very serious. They are still doing more tests on him and will know more in time. As for now that's all they know.”

“Is there anything any of us can do for now?”

“John, right now I believe being a good friend and sticking by him is all anyone could or would expect from you.”

When you get to Birmingham you can take my car and go see him if you want. I can send Mark out with one of the other drivers on a trip until you get back. I don't mind doing this, I like the kid too.

John thanked Mary as he got off the phone. He went over to the small table where Mark was sitting drinking coffee. “Is that coffee any good?”

Mark just grunted, “Uh huh,” and went on sipping on it. John went and got a cup then sat down with him.

Mark took a look at John, “You look worried, is something wrong?”

John explained what he was just told.

Mark apologetically offered, “I'm so sorry for your friend. Maybe he will be alright.”

They both sat quietly drinking their coffee.

“This is not exactly where I would like to have a family reunion,” exclaimed Mike as his grandparents came in to the room.

His grandmother went over and put her hands on his face then leaned down and kissed his cheek. His grandfather on the other side of the bed grabbed his hand and squeezed. He looked up at them and told them how much he loved them. They were always there for him from a child. Just their presence gave him joy.

He then told them, “I guess Susan has filled you in on what's going on now.”

His grandfather answered, “Yes, they say you have leukemia and may be able to treat it.”

His grandmother asked, “Is that true, Mike?”

Mike told them what they knew and when he got to the part about getting his brother and sister involved his grandparents faces dropped as they looked so strange at each other. Mike couldn't help but notice the look they had.

“What's wrong with you two? You look like someone has died. I'm still here and am going to fight this with everything I have to fight it with.”

They quickly smiled. “Of course you will as we will too.”

They asked Susan, “Have you had any supper, dear?”

“I'm okay. I ate at home earlier this afternoon.”

Mike jumped in quickly, “No she hasn't. She won't leave me long enough to go and eat.”

Mike's grandmother replied, “Susan, will you accompany us to the cafeteria? We haven't eaten either and would be glad to have you. I'm sure Mike's friend won't mind staying with Mike while we're gone.”

“Go on and eat, Susan. I'll be glad to keep Mike occupied and tied to the bed for you,” replied Bob.

“Okay, I'll go.”

They went through the line at the cafeteria each getting what they wanted then went to a table and all sat down. While they were eating Mike's grandmother looked over at Susan. “We did not want to bring it up in front of Mike without first letting you know and perhaps getting your input on something we may have to tell him.”

“Now what would you need to discuss with me you couldn't discuss with your own grandchild?”

His grandparents looked at each other. Susan could sense the concern in their faces and the tension in their voices.

Then his grandfather calmly remarked. “Susan, I’m afraid it’s the grandparent part that’s in question my dear!”

“Exactly what do you mean?” Susan asked nervously.

Mike’s grandmother spoke first, “Have you ever wondered why Mike's grandparents on his father's side never seemed to have much to do with him? How they seemingly ignore him and then how they always appear to cuddle only to his brother and sister.”

“I know it's a sore spot with Mike.”

He said he didn't know why, but they never seemed to like him as much or make as big a deal over him as they did Jenny and William. And ever since the wreck took his parents he felt they may have blamed him for the accident. But he's learned to live with it now. He has his own children and tries so hard not to make a difference between them.

“Yes and we do admire him for this,” said his grandfather. “But the problem is William and Jenny is not his brother and sister, at least not by blood.”

Susan sat back in her chair shocked, “What are you saying? That he has another biological father! Or mother!”

The grandparents looked at each other. The grandmother grabbed a tissue from her purse for herself and one for Susan.

Both! Mike was adopted as a baby. His adopted parents were our daughter Michelle and their son Richard. His parents didn't like the idea of them adopting a child and never seemed to accept Mike as theirs. Richard and Michelle were married for a long time and were told they probably would never have children. So they adopted Mike. As will happen so many times they had two of their own. But they loved Mike every bit as much as they did William and Jenny. They decided on Mike's eighteenth birthday they were going to tell him he was adopted while clearing the air about why the other grandparents acted as they did. Mike was so looking forward to his party, even his friends were there.

Of course you know on his eighteenth birthday we had his party at our house. We were all waiting for his parents to arrive from work when we got the call about the wreck. Afterwards it didn't seem important to disrupt his fragile world anymore.

As spiteful as Richard's parents are I suppose they didn’t have the heart to tell him either. Now here we are and it may cause everyone who doesn't know to have false hopes about Mike's treatment. In other words, if he needs something from a brother or sister we don't have a clue as to where to start looking. There are no papers known to us. No details of his birth, nothing at all. The only people on the face of this earth who would possibly have known are gone and left nothing behind we can use.

Susan started crying. “This had to have been a terrible burden to live with ever since his parents died. Are you sure there's nothing will shed light on his past?”

His grandparents simply replied, “There is nothing at all.”

Mark was driving along Interstate 40 in Arkansas around midnight when John climbed out of the sleeper. “Are you getting sleepy, rookie?”

“Not really, just enjoying driving other than this rough ass road here.”

“Yeah, makes it tough to sleep when you're bouncing around like a basketball. Is anything going on with the CB?”

“Not much,” replied Mark, “just the occasional come on back over driver or you missed me, come on back in, that sort of thing.”

Suddenly John looked around a little bit closer. “How fast are you going, rookie?”

Mark glanced down, “I’m running around seventy or so, why?”

“If you intend to keep your license and actually have a little money left from your paycheck someday you might consider slowing down and running along with the rest of the trucks here in Arkansas."

Shocked, Mark slowed down and fell back behind the truck he was starting to pass. "What's the problem here, John?"

John turned toward Mark. "This is one of the states absolutely love to nail a truck for whatever they can. Fines for trucks are always extremely high here and simply seem to be a revenue producer for them. You haven't noticed all the trucks running in line with each other?"

"Not until you mentioned it. Guess I'm lucky, huh?"

John sat back in the seat. "North Little Rock will be coming up in a while. We'll stop at the 76 where we will fuel up and get coffee."

Mark looked down at the gauges, "I think we have plenty of fuel to make it to Birmingham, but I could use a cup of coffee."

"We're not getting fuel because we need it. We're getting it because I don't want to pay road use tax to Arkansas."

Mark looked surprised, "What do you mean road use tax?"

"This is one of the states where you have to buy enough fuel to cover their road use tax or else stop at the Weigh Station and pay it then. In other words if you can't produce a copy of the fuel receipt where you stopped and bought fuel they will charge you the fuel tax on the miles you drove in Arkansas."

Mark shook his head, "It doesn't make sense to me. Do we do this anywhere else?"

"Not anywhere we run, only in Arkansas."

They stopped and fueled up the truck then parked. As they were walking inside a woman came up and stopped them, "You boys need some company?"

Mark took on a look like a kid in a candy store. "What do you have in mind honey?" as he looked her up and down.

She started to speak when John grabbed Mark by the arm.

“We don't have time for this kid and we’ve got to get some things done.”

Mark protested. “Hey, I'm a big boy. I can handle myself.”

“Go ahead then and be very sure of what you're doing. Things aren't always as they appear to be in this trucking life.”

Mark turned around and headed back to the woman, “Sorry about that. Now what were we talking about?”

“Would you like to have a little company?”

Mark looked her up and down, “It depends.”

She smiled at him, “It depends on what, driver?”

To which Mark told her, “On what it's going to cost me.”

Suddenly there was a big man who stepped out from beside a truck and started walking up to Mark. Before the man reached Mark the woman said, “I would say about sixty days in jail should do!”

The man told Mark he was under arrest for solicitation. “You have the right to remain silent,” as he read Mark his rights.

John just stood there smiling as Mark looked at him, “What's going on here, John?”

“Don't ask me. You're a big boy, you can handle it.”

John went inside to pay for the fuel and get a cup of coffee to go. He started back to the truck when the woman stopped him again.

John laughed out loud, “Now you've got to be kidding me. Surely you're not going to try it on me!”

She smiled, “No, I was just curious as to how you knew. I don't remember seeing you before so what gave me away?”

Number one, no hooker will ever walk up to you in the lot and try to do business with you. Number two, it's one on one and due to the chance of rape or getting her ass beat she will not walk up to more than one man. Number three, if she's working the lot she will stay as hidden as possible to keep from being detected, walking in the open places her in jeopardy of detection.

"Plus no hooker working a truck stop will look as though she just got in from Hollywood after finishing her last movie."

The woman blushed, "I've had compliments before, but this has to be the strangest."

They both laughed.

Then the woman asked John, "Do you think we scared the Hell out of him enough he might leave the girls alone now?"

"I'm sure he's scared!" replied John.

He's a trainee and new to trucking. In fact the way he acts he appears to be new to life itself. I can tell you it definitely would have scared me. But I never would have gotten caught up in it anyway since I don't mess with the trash out here. And to be honest I don't think he does either. I think he was just a curious kid who probably didn't have enough money for one anyhow. He's been out of work a long time and all he has on him is what's left of the seventy five dollar advance the company gave him.

The woman turned and motioned for the car. The policeman drove up with Mark in the backseat. She opened the back door and then told Mark to step out. He climbed out of the backseat and stood with his head down. She walked around behind Mark and unlocked the handcuffs.

She then looked him in the eyes, "You just don't have a clue as to how lucky you are. If it were not for this man standing here you would be sitting in the city jail right now! I don't expect to ever see you soliciting a hooker here or anywhere else ever again. Are we clear on this?"

Mark looked up at her with tears in his eyes, "Yes ma'am," then hung his head down again.

She then turned to John, "I'm going to release him to you. Of course this would be if you still want him."

Mark looked up at John. John just stood there in deep thought for what seemed an eternity. "The boss lady does have a lot invested in him right now." John scratched his head and thought.

Then John smiled widely, "If it not for this I'd say put his sorry butt back in the police cruiser!"

Both of the cops laughed, "You can go now. Be careful out there."

As John started to walk away the lady cop caught up to him and handed him a card with her name and number on it.

"If you ever get back this way and have a little time to kill give me a call."

John took the card and read her name. "Okay, Helen. I'll be sure and call. Thanks."

"By the way, you know my name. What's your name?"

"John. My friends call me Big John."

She started laughing hard patting her legs, "John! Now that's funny. I don't think I'll ever be able to forget my first JOHN you see."

The cops left as John and Mark went to the truck.

Mark was quiet as a church mouse until John asked, "You still want to drive? Or do you think you want to ride a while?"

"Believe I'd prefer to ride until I can get some feeling back in my body."

After a while Mark asked, "Were you going to leave mc back there?"

"Of course I was! You made your decision, I made mine."

"Then what made you change your mind?"

John just sat there and smiled for a long time. Then he started humming an old country tune. Soon there was a big grin slowly came on his face, "She was really cute, wasn't she?"

Mark sat in the dark then looked over at John, "Twenty two, John."

Puzzled, John asked, "Twenty two what?"

"Twenty two years old."

John snickered at Mark's comment. "It's Birdwell."

Mark glanced over at John, "Last name, huh?"

"Yeah and I'd appreciate it if you kept it to yourself."

John added, “I only tell the people who earn the right to know.”

“What are you going to tell Ms. Mary?”

“Exactly what is it I’m supposed to tell Mary?”

“About me getting arrested?”

“Did you get arrested for something kid?”

Mark sat quietly in the dark for a little while, “Thanks.”

“Don't mention it. And I do mean, don't mention it!”

The trip back to Birmingham was very somber. John drove along listening to the radio with an occasional smile on his face. It was just breaking daylight when they pulled onto the terminal yard in Birmingham.

John parked the truck then roused Mark, “You think you can make enough room in your car for me so that we can get some breakfast at Niki's?”

Mark climbed out of the sleeper, “I don't care if I have to throw my record player on the ground and leave it. I will make room for you after last night.”

John looked off into space, “I don't know what you're talking about. I would just like to get breakfast.”

“I'll be right back.”

They pulled into Niki's lot and walked inside. As they went through the line John noticed Mary sitting alone at a table eating. They walked over with their plates and asked did she mind if they sat with her. “Alright with me, after all it’s your reputations at stake.”

“Morning Ms. Mary, you look good today,” replied Mark.

John then complemented as well, “He beat me to it, but you do look good today, Ms. Mary.”

She looked at both of them, “I'm not even going to ask. I don't think I want to know.”

John looked at Mary awhile then noticed there was something different today. He simply couldn't put his finger on it.

He had to ask, “Is there something wrong, Ms. Mary?”

She smiled, “No, I'm just a little sad today is all. John, I would hope you of all people would know what today is.”

John sat there and was even more puzzled than before. Then it hit him, how could he forget since he was a party to the event.

“Today is one the anniversaries of the day I stood up with my best friend Hammer Lane. As his best man I witnessed him marry one of the most beautiful women in the world on a warm sunny day just like today.”

Mary's eyes started to sparkle as John recalled the wedding.

“I am glad someone is here to help me remember. You have always been a good friend to both of us, John.”

Mark queried, “Are you talking about the truck driver Hammer Lane. Man, he was like a legend at the truck driving school. Some of the things he did were just unreal. Even though they said it was wrong for him to do them of course.”

Mary listened intently, “What are you talking about Mark?”

John stepped in, “Don't blame the kid, Mary. You know who's spreading these stories there and it's only out of spite for losing you.”

“You can't lose what you never had, John! He should realize that.”

Mark sat for a while, “Just what's going on here? Who are you talking about?”

John explained, “One of the instructors at the school.”

He used to drive a truck for the company Hammer, Mary, and I was leased to. He had a thing for Mary and thought she felt the same way for him. She was only being kind to him because no one else could stand his ego. He felt he was the only real driver on earth and everyone else should follow his lead. Hammer had words with him several times and always let him know in no uncertain terms he was full of crap. Also, maybe he should find another way to make a living since he was going to hurt himself or someone else if he didn't.

Mary added, “I never gave him reason to believe I had any interest in him. And I always told him Hammer and I was to be married as soon as we got our own company started. But he just wouldn't listen and now it seems he's spreading lies about a man he never really knew and also one who can't defend himself now.”

“If you and John say so then it must be true,” replied Mark.

“Ms. Mary, why don't you go with me to Montgomery to see Mike? It will do you good to get out of the office and enjoy your anniversary. I'm sure Mike would be glad to see you. What do you say?”

“Why not, it may do me good to get out for a while? I think office can take care of itself now. I believe I will go. I do need to catch a few things up in the office before we leave though, if that’s alright with you, John?”

“Sure Ms. Mary, there is no hurry.”

Mark sat back and looked like a child someone had forgotten when John asked him, “You want to go too, rookie?”

He perked up, “Thought you'd never ask.”

The doctor came in and had a strange look on his face as he stood beside the bed. “We now know what we are dealing with and what it will take to fight it”

We must start treatment immediately since it has progressed further than anticipated. We need to start chemotherapy as soon as we have the right combination. This means we are going to need to test your brother and sister to see which is going to be the best candidate for donation.

“I guess we need to call them. William is living in Nashville and Jenny is in Atlanta. It may take a while to get them here.”

“No, that's not necessary. We can have them go somewhere where they live and submit for the tests. Then we’ll have the one who will be the best candidate simply come to Birmingham for donation."

"Birmingham! Why Birmingham? Can't we do this here in Montgomery?"

The doctor explained, "The closest facility for treating this type of leukemia is in Birmingham and that's where your best bet for a successful treatment will be."

Mike looked at Susan and they both agreed. Then the doctor walked out as Susan excused herself to go get coffee and walked out with him. When they were safely away from hearing distance of Mike, Susan told the doctor what his grandparents informed her. The doctor stopped in his tracks.

"You do know this will seriously affect Mike's chance of a successful treatment."

"Yes, I know. But will the shock and stress of this knowledge not affect Mike adversely as well?"

"I suppose you could be right. It could trigger more white blood cells for what the body perceives to be infection. What do you propose we do?"

"For now let's keep his being adopted a secret. Then maybe somehow we can find out where he came from and hope and pray he has brothers or sisters."

The doctor concluded, "I agree, though it may turn out to be the proverbial needle in a hay stack."

It also may be the only course we can take. I have a few people who may be able to help. See what you and the rest of the family can do. Even though you may not get along with them you should ask his other grandparents if they know anything. It's a long shot, but worth a try.

Susan went and got a cup of coffee and returned to the room. When she walked into the room Bob and Mike were already in deep discussion on how best to handle the move to Birmingham.

Susan angrily jumped in, "What do you mean the move to Birmingham. Why will we need to move to Birmingham?"

Bob explained, “I have seen patients on chemo while I was in the hospital and also how very weak they got after each of their treatments.”

It may not be a good thing to expect Mike to have to ride back and forth to Birmingham. In fact it could lessen his chances for remission. I will be more than happy to find a place close by to cut down on travel.

“You've done too much already, Bob. We just simply can't let you continue to shell out money we know we can never repay.”

“You just let me worry over that. Not you and Mike. You’re the only family I consider having. How do you think I could stand by and let you carry the burden alone?”

John, Mary and Mark were on their way down Interstate 65 to see Mike in the hospital. They were talking about the school that Mark attended.

Mary was telling John, “I didn't know Jim was telling stories about Alan and making him some sort of bad boy trucker to serve his purpose. Now this is just not right!”

“Who is Alan?” inquired Mark.

“Alan is Hammer's first name. Everyone just called him Hammer which is what he preferred. Of course Mary called him by his first name, Alan. I have to say she was probably the only one.”

“He was my husband so I guess I can call him whatever I want to, right?”

“I am not getting into this at all. Sorry I asked who Alan was. But now I know and I also know everything I was taught in the school may be suspect now.”

John glanced back over his shoulder at Mark who was sitting in the back seat, “Now that's not necessarily true. Your training is not what’s in question.” Mark was trying to understand.

That's just one instructor out of many. The others apparently know what they're doing. Don't think everything you learned was wrong. Just realize even though Jim was using Hammer to prove a point, it doesn't mean the point was invalid. In other words, what he used to get there may have been wrong, but the end result was correct.

Mary said, "Let's stop in Clanton at the Bar-B-Que house and get something to eat before we go on in to Montgomery."

Mike was sleeping as usual while Susan and Bob sat and talked about what they needed to do to accommodate Mike. Bob kept acting unusually nervous as they talked and Susan finally asked him, "What's wrong with you? You appear to be nervous as a hooker in church."

"Nothing at all, I just hate to see my friends in such agony."

"Bob, I've known you long enough to realize when something is wrong. So don't try to hide it, fess up."

"Would you mind if we discuss it later, now is not the time."

"Okay, but remember you owe me an explanation."

There was a knock on the door as John, Mary and Mark walked into the room. They hugged and started talking and then Susan shook hands with Mary.

"I'm so glad to finally meet you. I do have to say one thing, Ms. Mary. I may have to keep a closer eye on Mike when he's around you now. No one told me how gorgeous you are."

Mary blushed, "You've been hanging around truck drivers too long. How is Mike doing?"

Mike opened his eyes and looked around the room. Then he chuckled, "Have I died? Seems as though everyone's here to see me which must mean it's my wake, huh?"

Everyone laughed and started talking to Mike. After a while John looked around the room.

"Where's Bob?" There is now an empty chair where Bob was.

Susan glanced over at where Bob was sitting. “He was right there a minute ago. He's been here all day. Perhaps he went to get something to eat. I must say it's awful strange for him to just walk out like that.”

“I'll go find him. I wanted Ms. Mary to meet him,” John told her as started for the door.

He winked at Mary when he walked by who gave him a go to Hell look as he walked out. John went down to the cafeteria and saw Bob sitting at one of the tables. John got a cup of coffee then went to sit with Bob.

“Mind if I join you?”

Bob looked up. “Go ahead and sit down. You ain't getting any taller, John.”

John sipped on his coffee while watching Bob play with the food he bought. “Are you actually going to eat that? Or do you intend to peck it to death?”

Bob smiled, “I've got a problem, old friend.”

“What exactly is the problem you have, Bob?”

“The lady you brought with you for one.”

“You mean Ms. Mary? Now what kind of problem would you have with her?”

Bob looked at John a moment, “Do you know who I actually am, John?”

“Of course I do. Your name is really James and you're the tanker driver who was in the wreck which killed Hammer. I don't know why you changed your name, but I have to assume you have your memory back and will be able to tell me what happened now.”

Bob smiled then glanced toward John, “You have part of it right. I did get my memory back, but it was around ten months later. By then there were things just couldn't be changed without harming a lot of innocent people.”

Bob paused for a moment to reflect.

John sat and listened intently, “What do you mean things couldn't be changed?”

“John, do you remember your friend Hammer telling you he had been looking for his brother?”

“Of course I do. He was always looking for his little brother, Bobby.”

Bob sat and just looked at John for a long time as Bob stared back at him. Then all of a sudden John sat up straight in his chair. “It's you! You're his brother, Bobby. How did he find you?”

“Yes, the tanker driver was Hammer's brother, Bobby.”

The people who adopted him changed his name to James. But it was James who found Hammer. It seems they were looking for each other all these years when James found Hammer first. In fact they had planned on getting together that weekend to tell Mary. Then go and tell their little brother whom James also found.

John sat and could hardly believe what he was hearing. He then remarked, “Little brother! You mean there were three of ya’ll?”

“Yes, there were three brothers.”

Hammer didn't remember the youngest since he was only less than a month old when their parents were killed. All he could remember was Bobby, the middle boy who was about three at the time. It was only by a fluke of a chance Bobby found out about the youngest boy whose given name was Charles. His adopted parents renamed him Michael.

John sat and tried to take all this in. The more he heard the harder it became to keep it all straight. “So Hammer was killed before he got to meet his little brother, but at least he got to meet the one he was looking for all his life.”

“No, that's not what I said old friend. Hammer did meet his youngest brother.” John is getting totally confused.

“So he met him before the wreck,” trying to understand.

Bob grinned, "No, he met him almost two years later."

John was becoming more confused by the minute. "Now you're not making any sense at all. How would he meet his younger brother after he was killed?

Bob sat back with an odd smile on his face. It was a smile John had seen many times before.

"HOW CAN THIS BE? Hammer it's you! But how can this be?"

Hammer said, "James and I were going to Asheville. He'd never driven a large car before. He kept begging me to let him drive my truck. How could I deny his request after finding him?"

So I let him drive my truck and I drove his tanker. He wanted to take the short cut to Asheville through Mountain City. I tried to talk him out of it, but he said he was an old hand on the route and he would lead the way. John, he lived in Asheville and he wanted me to see his home. He wasn't married and his adopted parents died a few years before, but he was proud of his home. He was going to unload in Johnson City and I was unloading in Asheville. After he took his truck to his home terminal and I got unloaded in Asheville he was going with me to Birmingham. So here we are and about halfway to Mountain City when we went around the curve and there was a van broken down in the road. Bobby hit it then went off in the valley to the left. I went up the hill to the right trying to miss the van then rolled over and was thrown from the truck. After that the rest is just a blur for me.

"So when I was coming to see you in the hospital you knew who I was?"

"No, not for about ten months as I said and I do have to thank you for visiting me, but the whole time you thought you were visiting James."

"So when you started to get your memory back is when you stopped talking to me. I suppose I could understand that."

Hammer shook his head, "I may need to explain it better."

"John, I was starting to remember at the time, but keeping the truth from you had nothing to do with it."

You just don't know how depressed I became once I could remember James. I had a deep guilt to live with knowing I killed my own brother after searching for him my entire adult life! Now only hours after finding him I sent him to his death. That is what was going through my head at the time and consumed my every waking moment. You only stood as a reminder for me on each visit. I had so much guilt and anger inside me all I could think is why I am alive? I didn't want to continue, not because of the painful treatments, I simply wanted to join James! The thought of meeting Charles helped bring me around.

"I could see where my being there didn't help the matter. Of course I didn't know and selfishly I only wanted to know what happened to you so I could give Mary closure. When you left the hospital where did you go?"

"I went to Ashville and lived in my brother's home."

It took me a long time to come to peace with my part in the death of James. Before you even get started yes I know James made his own decision to drive my truck. I also realize the same thing could have happened if he were driving his own tanker truck since he was in the lead. I just had to work the guilt out on my own. The peacefulness of the mountain home along with the fresh mountain air and the items James had scattered around the house where he was searching for me seemed to ease my mind enough to come to grip with the situation. We never know when God will call us home. I learned to live each day as my last and try not to regret anything else I do.

"What is it with Mike and you and this thing about God you both have? Hammer, you know some of the things have happened to me and my family. You know my feelings on a God I feel turned his back on me and mine as far as I'm concerned. I just get so mad when someone mentions what their God has done for them. I just can't see it!"

"Yes you can, old friend. There is more than one way to see every situation. I could and probably should have been killed in the accident that took James' life. Why I survived and James didn't is a mystery. There is your answer, John."

"Perhaps you're right. It is a lot to take in all of a sudden. I will take another look at this God thing and try to see where I fit into this. Just give me some time."

"It's not up to me John. It's up to God and He has all the time in the universe. The question is how much time do you have?"

"Okay, I get your meaning. What about Mary. Why didn't you try to tell her what happened?"

"By the time I got my memory back, it was too late."

She had already filed for and gotten the insurance money and expanded the business. How would I explain this mistake to the investigators? Even worse, how would Mary be able to explain she was not involved in some manner and lose the business? And most importantly, how would we pay back the money that was already spent? No, it was far better to stay quiet while leaving everyone to continue than come out and destroy everything. I knew you would see after her and keep her out of trouble and she would be well cared for by you, John.

"I guess I can see where you have a problem with Mary being here. So what will you do now?"

Hammer shook his head, "That's not the only problem here."

John frowned, "So what else is there I don't know?"

Hammer simply responded, "Charles."

"Charles? Now who is Charles?"

"My little brother whose adopted parents renamed Michael is here in Montgomery."

John questioned, "What does that have to do with anything we're dealing with right now?"

Hammer just stared at John for a long time. Then suddenly John exclaimed, "No! Not Mike!"

Hammer nodded his head slowly as John sat in shock.

"So that's why you're so close to Mike's family. Do they know? Wait a minute. Do they even know he's adopted? Wait! No! He has a brother and a sister! Now I'm totally confused. This is going to take a while to sort out. How many people know about all of this?"

"Including you and me?"

"Yeah, I suppose so."

"Two!"

John was still reeling from the information he just received.

"If you don't mind John, you still need to refer to me as Bob until we figure out what to do here."

John agreed, "What are we going to do? It's going to cause a lot of emotions to overflow and a lot of anger among a lot of people. I think for now we keep it quiet and see what happens."

"Agreed and do we tell Mike and Susan? Or do we simply wait and see? But I somehow have to let the doctor know since I may need to donate bone marrow. John, the one thing I believe is better to do is for me to stay away from Mary. There's always a chance she may figure out who I am and cause problems. At least for now until I can think how to handle this, don't you think that's the best thing to do?"

John nodded, "Let me go back up to the room and join in. I'll tell them you got tired and went back to the house to sleep. Then Mary, Mark and me will probably go on back to Birmingham. Your secret is safe with me. I am glad to see you and glad to have you around again. I guess it's just going to be a little different than before is all."

The two men hugged and John went back up to the room.

As John walked into the room Mary and Susan were sitting in the corner deep in discussion on something concerning some shoes Mary was wearing. Mike was talking with Mark about trucking and in the middle of a story during Mike's own training period. John felt ashamed he would have to break this little group up and get two of them back to Birmingham.

"Okay everyone we need to be heading back to Smoke City before it's too late."

Mary hugged Mike then Susan, "I really hate to leave. These are my kind of people here. But I know you're right. We need to let them have some family time without us interfering."

John, Mary and Mark prepared to leave.

Susan thanked them for coming, "When we start going to Birmingham for treatment we'll expect to see you there. And we may take you up on your offer, Ms. Mary."

John asked Mary, "What offer?"

"We'll talk about it later."

On the way back to Birmingham Mary dropped a bomb shell on John. "No one in this car can repeat this and if they do I personally will put them through Hell, understood?"

John and Mark agreed.

"John, while you were gone I noticed Susan feeling really bad. I asked her to go with me to the restroom."

While there I asked her what was wrong. You know me, John. I'm going to find out. Anyway, after a lot of probing Susan told me she was just told by Mike's grandparents Mike was adopted and his treatment may be in jeopardy. They have no idea if Mike has brothers or sisters or where they may be.

Mark didn't know what to say since he didn't really know Mike or his family and John had to pretend really hard to be concerned with this new set back.

John questioned Mary, "What has Susan done so far? I mean has she told Mike or anyone?" John was gathering information to help protect the innocent at this point.

"She's told the doctor so far, but Mike doesn't yet know. She's not sure what to do and is thinking of keeping it quite while maybe getting an investigator on it to try and get information on Mike's real family."

John sympathetically added, "I hope she has luck finding out the information she needs. Now what's this offer you made to Susan?"

Mary smiled, "I told her they can stay with me while Mike goes through treatment in Birmingham. I also told her I would find her something to do in the office so she can stay close to Mike. Who is Bob leased to and do you think he would be interested in working with us?"

"Bob has his own rights from what I gather. I just can't see him leasing to a company. But I will mention it to him. Don't get your hopes up though."

John was starting to sweat a little at the thought of Hammer and Mary in close contact. Just how in the world was this going to work? He thought how odd this must be. Most of these people are related to one another and don't know it. This was so sad.

Bob had convinced Susan to go home for the night and spend time with the kids. She left Bob to stay with Mike that night. Mike was in and out most of the night which gave Bob plenty of time to think about his next move. Susan came in early to see what the doctor may have to say. Early that morning the doctor would come in to check on Mike. Bob excused himself and walked outside of the room and stood. Soon he could see the doctor walking toward Mike's room. He asked the doctor if they could have a private talk. They walked into a vacant room and the doctor shut the door.

"I'm sorry. I don't think I caught your name."

"I'm Bob Walker and I have something to tell you must be known."

"Bob, I assume this has something to do with Mike."

Bob tried to gather his thoughts to explain.

"Yes it does, doctor. Mike does not know it yet, but he was adopted as a baby and William and Jenny is not his brother and sister."

"Yes, I already know this which puzzles me as to how you do?"

"Then that makes two of us! How did you find out?"

"Susan told me yesterday. She told me Mike's grandparents informed her of the situation and asked me for help finding his biological family, if there are any."

"My God, I had no idea Susan knew. Then of course his grandparents would know. I didn't even consider that."

"Which brings us back to my original question which is how do you know of this, Bob? And what have you to do with it?"

Bob took a breath and explained the situation to the doctor.

"I just want you to know should the need arise I do know where Mike's brother is. You're looking at him."

Shocked, the doctor replied, "Exactly what do you mean?"

"I am Mike's brother only he doesn't know it."

Bob explained he found Mike a few years earlier and he made friends with him, but decided not to tell him because Mike didn't know he had been adopted. And still did not know. It made no sense to disrupt Mike's life just for his satisfaction. So he thought it best to keep it secret unless needed.

"Are there any other siblings?"

"Yes, a brother in between us, but he died in a truck wreck several years ago. Mike and I are the only ones left."

"How much do you know about your parents?"

"Hardly anything except the fact they were murdered when we were very young. I remember this much."

There is nothing more I know. I can't remember their names or where they're from or anything else. I didn't even know about Mike until my brother found me and told me. I was the oldest at around six years old. I had and still have a picture of my younger brother and me sitting in a chair. Mike was only about a month old when our parents were killed. So I had no knowledge of him. It was only through my younger brother I found out about Mike.

"So until Mike is informed I am to disregard what I've been told and continue with his treatment. If, and there is a strong chance we will, we need you for a bone marrow transplant you will be willing to donate. Is this what you are telling me?"

"Yes sir," answered Bob. "I will do anything to save my brother."

The doctor shook his hand, "I hope everything turns out well for you both. If you don't mind later today walk down to the lab and tell them you are there for a blood test for compatibility for Mike Turner and give them my name as the doctor in charge."

"Yes sir, I will. By the way, I too didn't catch your name."

The doctor gave Bob the most beautiful smile, "Just tell them Doctor Jim sent you. They will know who I am, Bob."

Bob was feeling better now since having his little talk with the doctor. Not wanting to waste precious time he went straight to the lab and had a blood sample taken. Then he decided to get a cup of coffee and give the doctor time to talk with Mike and Susan. After enough time had gone by he returned to the room. To his surprise Mike's grandparents were there. And along with Mike and Susan everyone was crying. He wasn't sure what he had just walked into, but apparently it was bad.

Susan looked up then ran over to Bob and hugged him. He held her for a while then asked, "What's going on here?"

Mike's grandmother explained. "We just cleared the air over some things Mike should have known a long time ago. We just couldn't let him go on without knowing the truth."

"Exactly what is the truth you're talking about if I'm not over stepping my boundary?"

Confused, Bob was starting to fear the answer.

Mike looked over at Bob with tears in his eyes, "They just informed me I was adopted. The man and woman I called mom and dad all my life were not my parents."

Bob, tearing up himself, "Now that's not exactly true, Mike."

Didn't they feed and clothe you, hold you when you cried, punish you when you did wrong, laugh when you were funny, cry when you were sad? In short, didn't they do all the things parents do to ensure growth, teach and protect you? I don't know what planet you live on, but in my book that's a parent. Plus from what I've been told very good parents at that!

Mike sat and thought for a while then asked his grandparents to come over to him which they did. He grabbed and hugged them. "I'm sorry. It really must have been quite a burden on you to have this knowledge for so long and never knowing if you would have to share it with me. You truly are my grandparents."

It was just about all Bob could take watching the scene play out before him. Susan was still holding Bob's hand when Mike turned to him, "As always Bob, you come to my emotional and mental rescue pointing out my faults just as a brother would do."

"I suppose if true then it would be because there is a reason for it, Mike. The reason would be I am your brother. I'm your oldest brother."

All of a sudden there was an eerie silence in the room. At that moment everyone except Bob stood there in complete shock. It was Mike's grandmother who first responded, "That's nice dear. You've known him long enough to feel as though he's your brother. I understand."

Bob smiled then walked over to her and held her hand. "But I really am his oldest brother. Same as you I could see no reason to disrupt and confuse his life simply for my own satisfaction. He was happy with everything as it was and I didn't feel I had the right to change it same as you."

Bob could only hope and pray he handled this correctly.

She started to smile as Bob turned back to Mike, “This has to be the strangest family reunion ever. Actually, it is also my first!”

They all laughed as Susan walked over to Bob, “I must say you are most definitely my favorite brother-in-law. Now I can tell you how much we all love you.”

Bob went and hugged Mike, “It will get even better.”

“What do you mean, Bob?”

Bob just looked around the room, “The family just grew by more than one.”

Excitedly Susan exclaimed, “That's right! You said you were Mike's oldest brother. He has another!”

Caught up in the emotion of the scene now playing out before him Bob realized he revealed too much without thinking it out. Bob took a moment and considered the ramifications and consequences involved if he were to reveal himself at this time. Perhaps being near Mary again rather than watching her from a distance gave him a false sense of security. Whatever the reason, for now he must remain Bob.

Bob dropped his head, “Yes, but I'm afraid he's already gone. He was killed in a wreck. I don't know any more than that.”

Mike looked over at Bob, “Then do tell how this family grew by more than one. Are you married and have children? Do you know where our parents are and why they gave us up?”

“No, I'm sorry to say our parents are dead.”

They died when we were very young. I'm not married nor do I have children. I was thinking of John. I suppose he told you the story of Hammer Lane's accident. I was the tanker driver and if not for John visiting me in the hospital and encouraging me to fight to survive I would not be here today. That's why I consider him a brother and I'm sure Mike and the rest of the family will also.

Mike looked at Bob confused, “Strange you should mention Hammer Lane.,” as he smiled at Bob.

Bob felt his body tense from the mention of his true identity.

"Did you know he was adopted and spent his life trying to find his brother?"

Shocked, Bob answered, "No, I didn't know. I never actually meet the man. I just happened to be behind him that day and have wished more times than you can imagine things could have worked out differently. Some things you can't do anything about as it's all in God's hands."

Mike lay there taking in the moment and realizing the true scope of his situation. A few minutes ago he was informed his whole life had been a huge lie. To make things worse he may not have a chance to defeat this infliction he now faced. Thinking of his wife and family it was becoming more than he could ever bear. Then into his life comes the one person who meant so much to him and his family. Bob came to their rescue much like a medieval knight on a white horse to save the day! He didn't know why, but he felt truly blessed.

Mike waved toward Bob through teary eyes, "Come give me a hug, big brother!"

Bob walked over and hugged Mike as only a brother can do.

"I love you Mike and together we can beat this. I just went to the lab for a blood test for compatibility. Soon we can get the ball rolling on a more aggressive treatment for your leukemia."

John and Mark had unloaded the steel they brought back from Tulsa in Birmingham that morning. They went back over to the terminal to check with dispatch and also see if there was any more word on Mike. John and Mark walked into Mary's office.

"Good morning Ms. Mary, how are you this fine morning," asked John?

"I take off for one day and come back to three day's work to catch up," as she shuffled through a stack of papers on her desk.

"Otherwise it's not a bad day. How is the kid working out, do you think he will be okay?"

"Yes he is so far. He's just a little short and has a problem getting to the load, tarps and such, but he will adjust and find his own way in time. Have you heard from Mike this morning?"

"No, I did miss a call while I was out in the shop looking over the maintenance records. My secretary said they did not leave a message, but rather would call back. So I don't know if it was about Mike or not."

"If you don't mind pass along anything you hear please. Not anything I can do for him right now so Mark and I need to get back to work."

"That will be fine, John. I will pass along to dispatch anything I find out or perhaps have you transferred to me when you call."

Then Mary turned to Mark, "Now you get out there with John and learn the ropes. I expect you to make me a very good hand quickly."

"I will Ms. Mary, don't you worry. And I do appreciate the motel room last night."

"That's okay. I don't mind at least until you get back on your feet and can afford your own place. Train hard and quick then I can put you in your own truck. Then you can sleep in it while off duty on the weekends."

"I will make you a good hand, Ms. Mary."

John and Mark left to load for Sweetwater, Texas. Mary watched as they walked out and considered if only Alan were still alive to see how far the business had grown. Of course when the business is all you have to concern you, naturally you put your all into it. But yesterday and with it being their wedding anniversary taught her perhaps there is life outside of the office. She couldn't remember the last time she sat with another woman and just talked with no purpose seemingly in mind. For so many years now her every waking moment had to be very serious and meaningful. Now there she was discussing an old pair of shoes she hastily bought at a thrift store. She simply could not remember the last time she just let go in this manner.

Perhaps John was right. It may be time to join the living again instead of hanging on to the dead. She knew Alan would want her to go on and enjoy life even if it meant with someone else. Which reminded her, what was the deal with this Bob that Mike and John wanted her to meet? And just where did he go when he could have met her? She giggled a little as a school girl. Maybe he was just a little shy. Well, at any rate she would get to the bottom of it if and or when Bob came by to lease in with her. She felt herself smile in a manner she had not in many years.

"Bob, can I get you to do me a favor this morning?" asked Susan. Bob sat up from the easy chair he was trying to sleep in at the hospital room.

"Sure Susan, what is it you need?"

"Mike has been worried about the car needing the oil changed. Do you think you can handle this for me?"

"Why of course I can. Is there anywhere in particular you want it done?"

"I'm not sure, Bob. We'll ask Mike when he wakes up."

Mike opened his eyes and smiled, "I heard you two plotting against me!"

Susan walked over and lightly slapped his cheek, "Don't start none, won't be none!"

Mike giggled, "The answer to the question is it doesn't matter where you have it done. I just want to make sure they use Valvoline oil and a Fram filter. It's what I have used ever since we bought it new. I don't want to change now."

"I'll get it done, Mike. The doctor should be in shortly. Think I'll wait until he comes in before I go get it done if that's okay with you," as Bob settled into the chair.

"That will be fine, Bob. Or should I say Big Brother? Such a wonderful sound to hear as I suppose it may take some getting used to."

It was then the doctor came walking into the room. He smiled and shook hands with everyone then winked at Bob.

"And how is everyone this fine morning?"

Mike was first to say, "Good morning to you also as it is a wonderful morning for my family and me today."

Puzzled, the doctor asked, "And why is that, Mike?"

"Because doctor, I found out I was adopted as a baby. I know it was a terrible burden on all who knew. Then as it seemed all hope of a successful treatment was lost I find out I have a big brother in Bob. I would say this is the best morning of my life, wouldn't you doctor?"

"Well now I have to agree with you, Mike. And Bob, I suppose it must be a relief to have the burden of long time secrecy out in the open, correct?"

Bob swallowed hard. "Yes it is, doctor. I suppose we can get started on the aggressive treatment since you now have a donor."

"Not just yet, Bob. I've not received the results from the blood work. It could be a few more days as I wanted another matter checked as well. But we shall soon know."

"Thank you Doctor Jim," as Bob shook his hand again. Then the doctor walked out of the room.

Susan then remembered, "Bob! What about Ms. Mary? You didn't get a chance to meet her yesterday. We wanted so much for you to meet her."

"I can't help that. Perhaps one day I will meet her. As for now we have much too much to worry over than if and when I meet Mike's boss lady."

Then Bob hugged Mike and Susan, "I will be back later. I have to get the oil changed for you and make a few phone calls to my customers."

Bob was starting to worry over their instance he meet Mary.

"Do you think you know how to get to Sweetwater, rookie?"

"If you're asking if I can read a road map, yes?"

"Well, let's get this rebar loaded and you can plot a course."

After waiting for two hours to load they were soon on their way to Sweetwater, Texas. As they were going by Tuscaloosa Mark reminisced on growing up there as a child.

I spent many a Saturday at the stadium during football season when The Crimson Tide had a game there, where I would sell game items to the fans as they walked by. I even met "The Bear" a couple of times before he died. Just a little hard to express the excitement I felt back then. Since Coach Bryant died seems the magic is just not there as before. I keep forgetting to ask Ms. Mary if Hammer Lane was related to The Bear.

"I wouldn't think so since Hammer was adopted and took his adopted parents name. As for whether his adopted parents were related to The Bear I couldn't tell you."

They stopped in York, Alabama for lunch. Mark asked John,

"Is the food any good here?"

"Guess you will find out very shortly, rookie."

"What can I get for you?" the waitress asked Mark.

"I believe I will have the hamburger steak special."

"That comes with turnip greens, lima beans and peach cobbler for dessert. Do you want corn bread or biscuits?"

"Corn bread I suppose and coffee to drink."

"And you?" looking at John.

"The same as him, but I don't want the cobbler."

"Go ahead and get it John, I can eat both!"

"Okay, go ahead and bring the cobbler too."

After the waitress brought their meals Mark asked John about Bob. "I noticed the man that must have been Bob as we walked into the crowd at the hospital yesterday. He is the one with all the scars and wearing the dark wraparound sunglasses, isn't he?"

"That would be right rookie, why do you ask?"

"Oh, I was just curious as to what happened to him. Do you know how he got injured?"

"Yeah, he was involved with a wreck where he was driving a fuel tanker."

The truck rolled over and he was thrown out and covered in fuel. The fuel caught fire and he burned for a long time before anyone could try to put him out. His body was burned close to one hundred percent which is a miracle he survived and even more so is he is able to work again. He has my admiration as he should have yours as well.

"Oh my God, I didn't know! That has to be one of the worst things I ever heard of. So what's his relation to Mike?"

"I'm not too sure other than they have been friends for a long time. Maybe we will know more later on."

John sat back and thought he better leave this situation alone and stay quiet about any involvement with Hammer, Bob, Alan or whichever name he would continue to use. Especially at the moment since he was not sure just where this will lead or who would be told what and when. It would surely be a long slow process to keep the innocents' safe since if not done correctly could bring civil and or criminal investigations to light.

After finishing their meals they left continuing west through Mississippi. Mark was driving along as John napped sitting in the passenger seat. John kept nodding around and waking up then staring out the windshield for a while until nodding off again.

"Why don't you go ahead and climb in the sleeper, John?"

"I'm alright sitting where I am and besides, I need to keep an eye on you for a while, rookie."

John thought they would never get to Bee Bayou Truck Stop in Louisiana. It was always hard to sit and watch someone else drive when it seems you work just as hard driving as they do plus watching and correcting them. But this would be worth it since it will be Mark's first encounter with Ursula.

"Oh, it's you again," said Ursula as she looked at John while she walked up to the table.

"What did you bring me this time?"

Then she glanced over at Mark, "Oh, fresh meat and so young and tender!" as she began rubbing her hands and smacking her lips.

"What in the Hell?" said Mark as he started to get back up from the table.

"Sit your butt back down son. I ain't done with you yet! Now what do you want to eat, we will get to dessert later."

"I believe you better listen to her, rookie. She sure seems to be taken with you for some reason."

"Oh my goodness!" as Mark's eyes widened, "John, who in the world is this woman?"

"My friend this would be Ursula and she is probably the best known waitress in this trucking world. Don't let her scare you, rookie. She really loves us all."

"You know I can't stand my eggs with the yellow runny like this, Susan. It just simply ruins the rest of the meal for me."

"I know Mike, but that's beside the point. If you don't try and finish the rest of the meal they will start looking for another problem. I will be sure and tell them once again to scramble your eggs."

If truth be known after the lengthy stay in the hospital this time it took very little to anger Mike. From the machines that were his constant companion to the round the clock nurses and staff who seemed to enter and exit at will. Bob was sitting in the corner easy chair with a light blanket pulled up tightly.

"Good morning doctor," said Susan as the oncologist walked into the middle of three tired, confused and very nervous people.

The doctor smiled and looked around the room.

"Good morning as well," he responded. "I have some results to share with you today. But first I must tell you a little about what I have and also what it will mean to you."

Confused, Mike responded, "OK, I don't believe we will be going anywhere soon, will we?"

They all laughed for a short time until the doctor held his arm up in a stopping motion.

"At least you do still have a good sense of humor, Mike. Let us hope it will carry you all through the ordeal ahead. First off the results from the bone marrow compatibility test are not an exact match, but are close enough we may be alright to proceed using antirejection medication. The second part I will need to go into detail with you in order for you to understand. Have any of you ever heard of deoxyribonucleic acid?"

"Deoxy what?" asked Mike as Bob and Susan each shook their heads.

"Okay, have either of you heard of or know anything about DNA?"

Again each one had a blank and completely lost appearance on their face. The doctor knew he had an uphill battle ahead in order to explain the second test he had a friend do for him.

"Alright, then let's start at the beginning."

To just simply tell you the results will confuse you more than the answers to the questions you will have afterwards. To begin with, Gregor Mendel is considered the father of genetics. In 1857 while at the University of Vienna he worked with plants and then discovered a substance called nuclein. In 1884, Richard Altmann found the substance only exists in the chromosomes of cells. He named this substance nucleic acid in 1889 and initiated what we now call DNA. We now know the human body consists of billions and trillions of cells and each carry our DNA building blocks for the body. Each person's DNA is different, yet certain characteristics will remain among relatives and also specific races of men.

While research is still ongoing at this time I have a friend in a research center can determine lineage or relative probabilities to a percentage of possibilities. What I am telling you is because of the uncertainty involved in Mike's and Bob's relationship I had my friend test each one's DNA signatures for compatibility. I don't have the written results in hand, but he called me and gave me the results as he felt I should know quickly. Before I go any further are there any questions so far?

Mike, Bob and also Susan took a moment and looked at each other. Mike was the first to respond.

"So if I understand you correctly you are saying your friend can tell if Bob and I are actually brothers. Since we both only have the word of others to rely on you decided to send samples to your friend to find out for sure, is this about right?"

"Yes Mike, which is the long and short of it. Bear in mind this is not a beyond the shadow of a doubt answer. The results are a percentage of possibility the highest percentage being 99.9 percent positive. The reason being is no two humans have the same DNA, not even twins. But the closer the relation, the higher the percentage, do you all understand to this point?"

"I believe you have explained it well enough, Doctor Jim," Bob answered.

"Now you understand I must ask each of you before going any further. Do you all agree you want to know the results at this time? I will step outside and let you discuss it among each other. Just come to the door when you have decided." Then the doctor walked out of the room.

Susan began with, "Mike, Bob, this is your decision to make. I love you both and could care less what some test will tell us. In fact we already know all we need to know."

"Bob, what are your thoughts right now?" Mike asked.

"Mike, I think we need to know for sure while we have the opportunity. Then there can be no doubt from here."

"Susan, tell the doctor to come back in," Mike instructed as he straightened up in the bed.

The doctor came back in and looked around at everyone.

"What is your decision?"

"We want to know, doctor," Mike told him expectantly.

"Very well, according to the DNA profile test you are indeed brothers."

Mike, Bob and Susan each collected in a group hug crying tears of joy as the doctor stood emotionless at the foot of the bed. After just a short time they stopped and noticed the blank stare of the doctor.

"You don't appear to be very happy with the results, doctor."

"That's because there is more I must tell you will leave you with more questions than answers at this time."

"We are brothers, isn't this what you just told us the test results are?" asked Mike.

"Yes, you are brothers. However, according to the DNA profile markers you each share roughly half the genetic markers. Perhaps in a few years we may know more, but for now it gives you a starting point."

"What do you mean a starting point, Doctor Jim?" pleaded Bob.

"I suppose I must explain in a more understandable manner, Bob. To make it a little simpler, Bob and Mike, according to the results you are half-brothers. You share a single parent and we cannot tell you at this time which parent!"

The End

About the Author

Same as my dear friend and editor Perry G. Green, I grew up poor in rural areas of Alabama. The odd thing was we never considered ourselves poor. We always had plenty to eat and many activities to occupy our minds. One such joy was sitting and listening to our elders as they told wonderful tales of their youth. We would hang on every word as they told of their many experiences growing up and giving us life lessons we took to heart. Family was and still is my primary concern. Unknown to the faithful listener the torch of responsibility would be passed as one by one the voices of old received their Heavenly rewards.

I do not consider myself to be a writer, nor does anyone else. I am however a story teller trying hard to continue the tradition set forth by my ancestors. Written words often fail to contain the true experience of past lives with the passion they were lived. Pictures only tell of a split second they represent and not the excitement surrounding the event. That is where the story teller completes the mystery, much as the photograph carried by Hammer Lane in this book.

I began my career in long haul trucking in September, 1984. For over thirty-one years I have witnessed many changes in our great country, the people and also the trucking industry. More changes naturally will take place in the future. Shortly after starting my career I learned the TV shows and movies of the time cast a misconception of trucking. I decided then someone must tell the true life of the long haul driver accurately. That is why I chose this time period for the first book. Together with the reader we will grow into what trucking has become today.

To my knowledge there has never been a book written nor movie or TV show filmed to portray the lonely and frustrating life of the long haul driver. Quite often cast in an unfavorable light and vilified by media I wish to bridge the gap between these dedicated men and women with their fellow citizens.

Drivers sacrifice so much to keep this Nation prosperous. My own experience left me regretful for lost moments as my loving daughter grew from a child to the successful woman she is today. I can never get that back nor can I make amends to her for not being there for her when she needed my guidance and support.

If nothing else perhaps the next time you see a truck driver rolling along the highway you will consider them as a fellow human being with the same desires for life and the love of their family as you. They only wish to support and grow their families.

Until next time hammer down and enjoy life as God intended. God Bless us all,

David Hurt

You are welcomed to follow us on Facebook. Look for the "Hammer Lane Express" page and also our blog site "hammerlaneexpress.me" as we heartily encourage readers to comment, remark, criticize and also share their own stories that could possibly be part of future editions. Also an audio book is in process for the future. Come aboard and enjoy the ride. See you there.